Discovering Grace on Appleton Ridge

Discovering Grace
on Appleton Ridge

An Adventure in Love, Forgiveness,
and Recovery on the Coast of Maine

by
WELDON M. CLARKSON

RESOURCE *Publications* · Eugene, Oregon

DISCOVERING GRACE ON APPLETON RIDGE
An Adventure of Love, Forgiveness, and Recovery on the Coast of Maine

Resource Publications
An Imprint of Wipf and Stock Publishers
199 W. 8th Ave., Suite 3
Eugene, OR 97401

www.wipfandstock.com

PAPERBACK ISBN: 979-8-3852-1456-3
HARDCOVER ISBN: 979-8-3852-1457-0
EBOOK ISBN: 979-8-3852-1458-7

VERSION NUMBER 040424

Contents

Introduction,
A Word from the Author

I fell in love with the Coast of Maine as a teenager attending a private academy in Glen Cove, Maine. I grew to appreciate the sunrise over Penobscot Bay, helping pull lobster traps on the "Laura" and going to church... or "*chuch*" with my friend Kerwin Kramer. With his yellow Chevy Impala convertible, this fun-loving man would make a weekly run to Union Maine loaded with boisterous teenage boys seeking an escape from the rigors of academia and regimented dorm life.

Today I am a white-haired grandfather, having resided in half a dozen countries and visited thirty-some others. Although nearby Florida beaches are attractive, my heart longs for Penobscot Bay. This inexplicable longing has hounded me since boyhood, and will no doubt fill my dreams until I retire in a pine needle-covered cabin between Damariscotta and Blue Hill. In the meantime, join me in discovering the beauty of Downeast, its unique accent, and the people who inspired this story. Central to our story is a white, clapboard church where God's life-changing message of love and forgiveness is spilling out onto mid-coast Maine. To do this story justice, I have included the Downeast Maine accent. As it can be confusing for visitors, let's start with a couple of words that need some explanation:

Flatlander: Noun, A general term to describe someone not from Maine; someone from away; an "*outta-state-a*," a "*flatlandah*."

Ayuh: Means yes, or at least an acknowledgment from a Mainer. *Havin a good day? Ayuh.*

Chapter 1

A Divine Appointment on the Breakwater (October 2013)

Harold and Liz walked hand in hand on the breakwater stretching from Jameson Point out into Rockland Harbor. At the end of the 4300-foot granite structure sits a white and red brick lighthouse. Completed in 1902, it is owned by the City of Rockland but is maintained by the U.S. Coast Guard. Ships, out as far as seventeen nautical miles, have trusted their lives to Rockland light. Made of 700,000 tons of local granite squares the breakwater appears deceivingly flat, however, walkers soon discover it can be treacherous when wet. Local athletes consider running on the breakwater a challenge not to be taken lightly. One slip on the wet, uneven surface and you could easily break your leg. Today, however, the surface was dry, allowing the walkers to take in the beauty of Penobscot Bay at their leisure.

Seagulls squawked loudly and circled overhead, hoping to receive a treat. "They are like flying dogs . . . begging for a treat," said Liz. Harold laughed and pointed to a red and white lobster boat chugging its way in from the cold blue waters. "That's Bill . . . McCann or McMann . . . I think. These crazy lobstermen fish all year . . . I don't envy them on a cold day like today. If they ever fell overboard with their big boots and thick clothing, they'd be goners in that freezing water. You'd be numb before you could ever swim to the boat. I met him the first day we landed here last fall." They watched the lobsterman work for a while. They soon grew tired of trying to focus on the boat which bobbed up and down with the waves. Bill was outside of the breakwater and the waves were surprisingly high. To the west, inside the rock wall, it was almost as calm as glass. Harold thought to

1

himself: "Well, duh . . . I guess that's what a breakwater does . . . it breaks the waves!"

Soon they arrived at the lighthouse. The last time they had ventured out here the foghorn let loose with a mighty "Bhaaaaaaaaa" catching them both by surprise. Harold had laughed loudly as they scampered out of the direct sound blast and into the shelter of the backside of the lighthouse. Liz poked him in the ribs exclaiming, "That scared the snot out of me." Harold screwed up his face and replied, "Really Mrs. Tuttle . . . Ladies don't talk that way!" "Oh, come on! I saw you raise a foot off the ground when that horn blew!" Admitting she was right, Harold just grinned. They were all alone out here and the wind whipped at them turning their noses and ears bright red. It was warm enough walking in the sunshine, but she recalled Harold's comments about what happens to anyone who should fall overboard. The North Atlantic was to be respected.

They had learned about respect for the ocean as Bernie had trained them in boat operation, navigation, and marine safety. Her mind went back to last fall when, on the Baby Titanic, Bernie had made them wear life vests and had distributed safety training brochures from the Coast Guard, insisting they "read and memorize." "The ocean" yelled Bernie over the growl of the engine, "is a wonderful friend. You will have a great time out here . . . but take the buoys and markers very seriously. I have seen the coasties pull one too many bodies from this bay! People get out heyuh . . . they don't pay attention . . . they go too fast . . . get too close and then it's all over. And then theyuhs beyuh. People get to drinkin' and they chug down a six-pack . . . and all of a sudden they become wicked smat . . . I tell ya . . . beyuh makes people smat . . . so smat it kills 'em!" Liz thought about Bernie's lecture, remembering it almost verbatim.

Her attention was drawn back to a large two-level ferry heading out the mouth of the harbor, tooting its horn then gently turning north. Watching the boat with interest, Harold spoke, "Must be headed to Vinalhaven and North Haven . . . maybe even Matinicus."

As they made their way to the south side of the lighthouse the pair suddenly became aware they were not alone. Down, almost to the waterline, sat a single, silent, unmoving individual. "I hope they're all right," said Liz with a concerned look. Squinting to make out the details, Harold motioned Liz to stay where she was. "Do you have your cell in case we need to call 911?" Liz nodded emphatically. Climbing down the large granite blocks, Harold realized he was beginning to slip on the slimy seaweed covering the rocks facing the open water. Daylight was fading and the tide was rising. Whoever was sitting there needed to move or they would be in real danger. Walking nearly one mile to Jameson Point would be next to impossible as the wind whipping across the breakwater would cause wet clothing to freeze, dangerously lowering your body temperature. Squinting into the blackness Harold yelled "Hello!" No response.

Waves crashed into the rocks below sending a freezing spray that coated his jacket and stung his ungloved hands. Drawing nearer to the huddled figure he yelled again. This time the figure heard him and turned toward him with a startled look. "Are you all right?" shouted Harold over the crashing din of the waves. Drawing near, he saw a small person, perhaps a boy . . . or maybe a small woman, trying to get to her feet. As she struggled, the wind sent her off balance and she grabbed wildly for the rock behind her. Hal reached out. "Here, take my hand." Liz watched from above wondering if she should call 911 or just wait to see how things developed. After what seemed like an eternity, Harold's head appeared above the granite . . . and then, there he was . . . all of him, thank God . . . and he was pulling a young, very frightened woman up over the edge. Liz hurried toward them and met the pair as they made their way around to the shelter of the building. "Come in here!" shouted Harold as he yanked hard on a creaking black metal door. The lighthouse, now automated had not had a light keeper since George Woodward had retired in 1945. Wisely, the Coast Guard had provided visitors access to one windowed room in case of emergency. Equipped with a table and chairs and somewhat dim lighting, the room sheltered the three from the wind and cold.

Taking a seat, the shivering girl pulled back her ice-covered hood. Harold's eyes grew wide but did not speak. "Hey, don't I know you?" asked Liz. Harold leaned forward. "The Fungus Amungus, you served us there and then you led us to our cabin . . . Amanda . . . no Samantha . . . that's it! Samantha . . . What in the name of love were you doing down on the rocks? The tide was coming up fast. You could have died . . . frozen to death." Samantha nodded in silence. She was cold, shivering and her mascara had run down her face. She had been crying and she was nearly hypothermic. Samantha explained that she had come out here to be alone . . . to think and had fallen asleep. Liz and Harold looked at each other and knew what the other was thinking. There was something not right about her story, but this was not the time and place for an interrogation. What this girl needed was some hot soup . . . and quickly. Harold took his shot. "Look, Samantha, let us help you get warm, or you could be in real trouble. You need to get moving and get your blood flowing. You need to raise your core temperature. You are white as a ghost. So, here's what I propose. I'm fine . . . so you put my coat over you and walk with Liz back to Jameson's point. I'll drive your car and you and Liz come in our car, we will get some hot soup into you. I know just the place.

Thirty minutes later, the trio arrived at the Tradewinds restaurant. Soon Samantha Gifford was spoon-first into a large steaming bowl of chowder. Samantha's cheeks grew rosy, and she grew more talkative. Harold studied her thinking "Someday, I am going to find out what in the dickens she was doing out there on the rocks!" He knew in his heart this was neither the time nor the place for that discussion. An hour and a half later a happier and warmer Samantha turned right onto Main Street, her old green Subaru disappearing from view. Harold tried to recall if Samantha had ever told them where she lived. He only knew it was north of Camden . . . somewhere between Lincolnville Beach and Belfast. He would find out . . . and he would get to the bottom of this. One could not be expected to save a life from certain peril and not be informed as to the circumstances that led this young woman to make such a foolhardy decision.

Turning left onto Highway 105 toward their new home in Appleton, Liz spoke quietly, "Hal, what would have happened if we hadn't walked out on that breakwater today . . . and when we did?" Harold looked at her shaking his head. "You know, Pastor Harold Tuttle . . . I believe we had a divine appointment today and you and I have yet to figure out why." Looking through the windshield Harold spoke calmly: "You know Hon, I used to think that being a minister was all about Sunday . . . and preaching . . . but there sure is a lot of Kingdom business in between Sundays!"

Lying in bed, Hal watched the ceiling fan spin as his mind went back to how it was that they had come to live in Maine. It had been a convoluted and unexpected path. Suddenly let go from a stellar career with one of the best public relations firms in Minneapolis, he and Liz now found themselves discovering life and ministry on midcoast Maine.

Chapter 2

A Wicked Good Offah! (July 2013)

Picking up the phone, Liz began to talk. The voice on the other end was both familiar and friendly, bringing a smile to her face. Pastor Jim always had a way of making Liz feel better. He had, without question, a heart for people. His voice was not hard to recognize. Ten years ago, Pastor Jim and Debbie Dinsmore had accepted the call to Faith Community Church. Coming from Rockland, Maine, the Dinsmore's had found Minneapolis as foreign to them as Singapore.

It seemed the oddest blend. One of the coldest cities in North America had managed to build miles of glass, and heated skywalks between the downtown buildings making the city look like a giant Gerbil tube world. Maine had attracted only a handful of black settlers making Maine an almost white state. Jim always figured the black community didn't like the cold . . . that was until he came to Minneapolis.

The "Twin Cities" of Minneapolis and Saint Paul boast a unique blend of old-world Scandinavian conservatism . . . thrift, and simplicity . . . while home to the mecca of shopaholics, the 2.5 million square foot Mall of America. On a cold winter evening, there could be no more surreal adventure than strolling through the enormous complex. One cannot walk all of its four levels in one day. Walking around the outer edge will cause you to break out in a sweat . . . after all, it is a several-mile hike around. The center boasts a full-size amusement park and in the underground section, a world-class aquarium.

When minus twenty outside, one can shop in comfort, take in a movie, or sample any one of perhaps a hundred food vendors or world-class restaurants. If an item you are searching for cannot be found at the Mall of America, it may not exist. Specialty stores sell everything from Vikings football memorabilia to hot sauce to designer-label clothing or high-end, gold-plated ink pens. With twenty thousand parking spots there is generally lots of parking...you just need to brave the Minnesota winter to get there. This grandiose structure on the edge of town remained an enigma to Jim Dinsmore.

"I suppose it's Harold you want to talk to?" Liz queried. She always found her pastor's Maine accent amusing. The closest she had heard to the real thing was the pitiful Maine accent attempted by the late Tom Bosley, sheriff of the fictitious Cabot Cove on the television series called Murder She Wrote. Now and then, she would hear some sort of accent on "Newhart" although that was supposed to be Vermont . . . although Maine, New Hampshire, and Vermont accents can be similar. Recently she had commented to Harold that Norm Abrams, the host of PBS's The New Yankee Workshop had an accent close to Pastor Jim's.

Later that night the Dinsmore's sat facing Hal and Liz in their living room, anxious to help them put together an action plan. "I am serious," insisted Pastor Jim "This would be the perfect place for you and Liz to unwind for a few weeks. It's late summer and the tourists will mostly be gone and there is no place on earth more beautiful than Penobscot Bay, Maine!" Pastor Jim was doing his best to convince Harold and Liz to get away for a few weeks . . . clear their heads and spend some time talking, boating, walking on the beaches and trails, sampling local seafood . . . and trying to get some clarity about the next steps in their life.

Liz's questions were practical, her concerns being about Walter, their loving and loyal poodle, and leaving their house unoccupied. "Not a problem Liz, Walter will love our cabin. There will be lots of room for him to run and the deacon board is ready to stop by your house here and check it thoroughly once a week. I'm serious . . . you haven't lived until you have sat in our Adirondack chairs with a fresh mug of Joe . . . watching the sun come up over Penobscot Bay!" In the background, Harold broke out into "The best part of waking up is Folgers in your cup." "Oh, come on!" said Liz . . . this is serious, Harold. Grinning ear to ear he looked at his visitors . . . lifted his mug of coffee and proclaimed "*Ayuh.*" Pastor Jim roared with laughter and then paused, looking curiously at Harold. "Is that a yes?" Harold looked at Liz . . . and as if speaking some silent language only they knew . . . they both looked at their pastor and nodded.

"Alright then!" bellowed Jim. Give me a piece of paper and a pen. I will have to draw you a map . . . it's sort of out of the way . . . and not marked well. I will call Bernie tomorrow. He'll make sure the power and water are turned on, the lawn gets mowed, and Betsy will put clean sheets on the bed and stock the fridge with some basics. Hey . . . I'll get her to buy a couple bottles of Moxie." Liz looked suspiciously at him. "What in the world is Moxie?" Jim broke into a broad grin and began to speak. The "Reverend" Dinsmore, having graduated with honors from Gordon-Conwell Seminary, very rarely let himself slip into his native dialect . . . however when it came to explaining about Moxie to a "flatlander," he would let down his hair and *"Let 'er rip like a Mainah."* To Liz and Harold's amazement their pastor broke into the thickest coastal Maine accent they had ever heard: *"Why my deah theyah ain't nothin as maavaless as a cold Moxie. It's a might like a root beah . . . but bettah . . . and yes suh . . . made right in New England . . . you've just got to try a cold Moxie!"*

The couples spent the evening going over details and suggestions of where to go . . . what to eat . . . where to buy groceries . . . what to do if the septic got slow . . . what local to ask about where to catch "Blues" off North Haven. Then came the keys . . . one for the chain across the drive, one for the cabin, one for the well and pump house, one for the tool shed, and one for the boathouse. In the boathouse, they would find the key to "Baby Titanic" a 21-foot fiberglass Boston Whaler. "Don't worry," said Jim, "Bernie will show you everything you need to know about boats and navigating. Just remember when you see the buoys "Keep the red on your right upon return . . . Green on your left." Don't get out of sight of land, don't stay out after dark, always check your gas, always have your cell phone, stay away from the rocks, and always smile and wave at the Coasties."

"The what?" inquired Liz. "The Coasties . . . the Coast Guard. They're good people . . . and have saved many a stupid tourist who ignored the rules. Locals rarely get into trouble . . . its usually rich tourists from New Jersey and such. When you get to Rockland, there's a Coast Guard station down by the pier . . . right behind the Wayfarer Motel. Stop in and say hi to my cousin Frank Sullivan . . . and call him sir. He is the station commander. He's a good man and he will keep an eye out for you. Unfortunately, the Coasties have towed in the "Baby Titanic" a couple of times . . . but they're really good about it. I lost the prop when I hit a rock fishing off Butter Island . . . they saved my skin. Ask for a boating safety guide. That and some common sense and you should have a blast!"

The events of the day had left Harold and Liz exhausted. As they lay in bed staring at the ceiling, their thoughts spun like the ceiling fan silently churning above them. What in the world would they do fifteen hundred miles from home . . . in a cabin overlooking Penobscot Bay, Maine . . . and a boat? Are you kidding? No doubt it was a generous offer . . . or as Jim had said . . . *"A wicked good offah."*

Now, in late August they were on their way and the dream was becoming a reality. The first nine states they transected went without a hitch although the almost four hundred miles across New York took almost a whole day by itself. Early on the third day, the burdened white SUV headed north from Portsmouth, New Hampshire. Cresting the bridge that links New Hampshire and Maine, the morning sun sparkled on the cobalt-blue water. Liz squinted through the side window and said "Wow . . . Look at that beautiful sunrise!" "The sun rises in the East . . . and sets in the West!" added Harold. "California has great sunsets . . . but if you like to get out of bed . . . New England's just the ticket!"

The East Coast sunrise had just revealed itself in all its glory. There was no question Minnesota was beautiful, with verdant forestland in the north woods, the Boundary Waters State Park, the golden wheat fields of the western prairie, and the high green bluffs of the Mississippi Valley. However, watching the sun rise over the rocky Atlantic coastline was a new and wondrous experience. As good fortune would have it, this would be the first of many New England sunrises they would enjoy.

Across the bridge, a large green sign proclaimed: "Welcome to Maine . . . the way life should be." "Hey, Walter . . . want to go on your leash?" "Well, if he doesn't . . . I will!" chuckled Liz. "That coffee we had on the Mass "Pike" wants to find a new home. So, while Liz disappeared into the large modern welcome center, Harold and Walter explored a grove of tall Maine Pine trees. Walter sniffed at pinecones the size of Idaho bakers and, after christening a dozen of the giant coniferous trees, was content to be tied to a light pole as he chewed lazily on one big pinecone.

Coming out of the restroom, Harold found Liz busily discussing their travel plans with the cheerful freckled man behind the counter. While Harold poured himself a cup of coffee from a pot labeled "Leaded," his eyes scanned the copious display of travel brochures. They all seemed to have one united goal . . . to empty your bank account. "Visit the Kittery Discount Outlets . . . Brand names are discounted by up to 70%...Visit world-famous L.L. Bean in downtown Freeport, Maine . . . your shopping paradise . . .

visit DiMillos Floating Restaurant, on the waterfront in Portland . . . ask about our double lobster special."

Seeing Harold with an arm full of brochures, the rotund travel guide bellowed *"Well . . . yessuh . . . I'd say yowah in fowah some mighty nice weathah this week! That theyah weathah man on the Mount Washington station says it's gonna be hottah than Hades all through Sunday . . . so you and the misses heah won't be needin no sweatahs!"* Reaching under the counter he brought up an official State of Maine map. Pressing it into Liz's hand, he grinned broadly and exclaimed *"And, welcome to Maine!"*

About forty minutes later, Harold pulled onto an exit ramp announcing "Portland, South Portland, 495 N, Bath-Brunswick, Points North." After working their way through Portland's "Old Port" district with its many unique shops and gourmet restaurants, they crossed the enormous bridge linking Portland to South Portland and followed the signs that read "To Portland Headlight, Cape Elizabeth."

The highway wound its way around the rocky coastline, past elegant turn-of-the-century homes with high peaked rooflines hiding in the shadows of the tall pines. They rolled gently past brick and stone manors nestled on little tails of rocky shoreline. The blue ocean crashed into the rocks sending a salty white spay skyward. Gardeners bent earthward, fastidiously scooping dirt and preening greenery. High wrought iron gates held the common folk at bay with video cameras and carved wooden signs reminding all who passed that this was indeed "Private." As Harold and Liz passed, a large green gate swung open, and a polished seven hundred series Beemer slipped effortlessly onto the roadway. In mock aristocratic demeanor, Harold looked at Liz, held a white Bic pen between his fingers, and, with pinky extended, proclaimed "Muffy my dear . . . you and I simply must buy some prime real estate along this cozy little promenade." Laughing, Liz replied with equal mockery "Oh that would be just fab darling...let's say you get a job first!"

With the summer crowds of tourists dwindling, there was ample parking and room to walk at the lighthouse. The Portland Headlight overlooking beautiful Casco Bay is reputed to be the most photographed lighthouse in the world. Never has a calendar of Maine, New England, or lighthouses ever gone to print without the "Headlight." Those who see the lighthouse for the first time could be easily convinced that the green cottage nestled up against the tower must be the home of the venerable lighthouse keeper. That is, unfortunately, no longer true. Long ago the gas-fired wick and prism were replaced with an electric light source controlled by telemetry and electronic sensors. Data is fed to an offsite control center of the United States Coast Guard. Up until the early nineties, the Coast Guard housed a small contingent of technicians in the quaint cottage.

The wind blew Liz's hair, and she squinted as she surveyed what must be one of the most breathtaking views on the planet. Seagulls squawked overhead, colorful lobster trap buoys bobbed near the rocks, and over the roar of the waves you could distinguish the "tuff, tuff, tuff" of an old lobster boat chugging slowly along, tending to its business.

Harold, minding the sign "All dogs must be leashed" had Walter in tow as he approached the mesmerized Liz. She turned to them adjusted her cap in an unexpected gust and yelled over the crash of the waves "Wow . . . this place is awesome!" "Right you are!" replied Harold. "What would Pastor Jim say? *Godjus . . . yessuh . . . just godjus!*"

Heading north on route one, they entered Freeport, the home of one of the world's most successful catalog retailers L.L. Bean. "Oh, this is so cool Hal . . . I have heard about this place for years . . . and now here we are." Along Main Street, Bean's multiple stores and outlets sprawled across the town. Starting in an old two-story general store with a pot-bellied stove smack dab in the middle of the creaky hardwood sales floor, Beans became the store of choice for sportsmen and outdoorsmen the world over. Products from Beans have been carried to the top of Everest and into the deepest Amazon rainforest and well frankly who knows where? L.L. (Leon Leonwood Bean) invented a hybrid waterproof shoe/boot called the "Maine Hunting Shoe." Its bottom is formed like a rubber boot with a leather upper sewn on it. Handmade in a factory down the road from the store, the famous "Hunting Shoes" come in all heights and warmth levels. For Maine hunters, it created the first opportunity to trudge through wetlands for hours without getting their feet wet. Although this boot made Beans famous, they soon launched into clothing for the entire family as well as an amazing product line of everything the gentleman outdoorsman might need for his cabin, camping expedition, canoeing, safari, or fly-fishing trip.

Pulling into a parking spot, Liz asked: "Do you suppose they're open?" "Well, the brochure I looked at said they are open twenty-four hours a day . . . seven days a week . . . three hundred and sixty-five days a year!" explained Hal. Liz looked his way and spoke one word: "Unbelievable!"

Once inside, they were like kids in a candy store. While Liz tried on sweatshirts and khakis, Harold studied the hundreds . . . if not thousands of varieties of hand-tied fishing flies, rods, reels, hip waders, and associated gear. It was almost too much to fathom. Fly fishing had always intrigued him. It seemed like a more scientific, cleaner way to catch fish. He had always disliked baiting hooks . . . but where to start? A kindly clerk with half glasses and a tan canvas vest spoke up: *"Say . . . mistah . . . theyah gonnah catch some trout in the trout pond in ten minutes . . . you should go watch. They don't hurt the trout any . . . they use baabless hooks and they always let'em go. They got some big dudes in theyah!"* Harold thanked him and began searching through the ladies' clothing racks for Liz. He could hardly believe the enormity of this store . . . with a stocked trout pond right on the main floor! This was too much.

After taking in the demonstration, Harold and Liz left burdened down with several large green bags. As they continued north on route one, Liz extolled the virtues of buying sensible, solid cotton clothing for their upcoming coastal sojourn. Harold gave her a knowing glance and with a smirk on his face practiced his newly learned colloquialism . . . *"Ayuh!"*

Chapter 3

Francophone Follies

Heading out from *"Freepot,"* U.S. Route One winds north a few miles inland, running parallel along the coast giving only brief teases of the ocean view. At Bath, a high bridge affords a view of the Kennebec River . . . dredged deep enough to permit gargantuan Navy ships enough draft to come and go from the Bath Iron Works shipyard. Further north in Wiscasset Route One crosses the Sheepscot River offering a postcard view of lobster tenders and sailboats at anchor. Along Route One, lobster boats and Boston Whalers look strangely out of place sitting in driveways and front lawns. The casual passerby might wonder . . . but the locals know that the ocean is but a short distance east through the thick coastal woodlands. It is not until the town of Rockland that travelers are treated to a full-on view of the Atlantic in all of its glory. It is here, in this fishing industry hub, that route one "T bones," forcing you to head north or south. Either direction rewards your patience with a view of beautiful Rockland *"haabah"* complete with granite breakwater and red brick lighthouse.

Much to Liz's delight, Harold managed to find a parking spot right in front of the Down East Goose gift shop. "You browse while I take Mr. Goofydog here for a tinkle. This was just one of Harold's many bizarre and affectionate names for Walter. When Liz had brought the pup home for the first time, she had announced that his name was to be Walter. From the beginning Harold was adamant that Walter was an appropriate name for a postmaster . . . but not a poodle. Instead of arguing the point, Liz suggested that he call the dog whatever he liked . . . but she would call him Walter. Well-tempered Walter soon learned to respond to whatever name Harold would concoct: Mr. Goofydog, Fuzzhead, Furball, Dog Blunder, Skruffydu-falous, Poodlekadoodle, and Biscuitbreath. Any number of names worked well for Walter as it seemed more to be the tone of Harold's voice than the actual words that had an effect. Harold's affectionate tone let him know that there might be an ear scratching . . . a belly scratch . . . a bone . . . maybe a walk. But when he was bad . . . like when he chewed on the TV remote, Harold would indeed call him Walter.

Temporarily tinkled out, Walter walked with Harold along the pier overlooking a fleet of working boats. These rugged boats called "Tenders" were generally rugged, short quite wide with low gunwales. Some had traps stacked on the rear decks and some were cleaned off, mechanics popping their heads in and out of engine access wells as they worked on maintenance and repairs. Making the craft as seaworthy as possible is a high priority as losing power near a rocky coastline can spell disaster and possible death to the lobstermen. Many of the boats were wooden with simple equipment while some of the larger, sleeker fiberglass vessels boasted sophisticated radar, satellite positioning equipment, and high-powered UHF radios.

At the mouth of the harbor, Harold could see a red and white tender gently rolling with the swell as it made its way back in for the night. As it grew closer, Harold noticed the boat was older, but in pristine condition. The big cast iron single-piston engine made the distinctive tuf . . . tuf . . . tuf he had heard once before. To his amazement, the boat slid right up to the slip where Harold and Walter stood.

Without any hesitation, the tall captain in yellow slickers, boots, and a Yankees baseball cap threw a large loop of rope at Harold's feet. Both Harold and Walter jumped back in amazement. *"Hey theyah . . . don't mind loopin that over the pilin, do ya?"* Grabbing the heavy, worn rope, Harold dragged it a few feet and looped it over the thick wooden piling. As he did so, the young man jumped from the rocking boat onto the dock and tied the rope from the stern.

"Hey thanks," said the young man as he grasped Harold's hand. His hand was as tough as leather and tanned deep brown. Harold secretly wondered how many hours of his life he had spent in the sun and wind on the salt water. For a moment, Harold thought about all the hours he had spent behind a desk typing on a keyboard. As the man let go of his hand, Harold felt a flash of embarrassment at his soft, white hands. *"Bill McCann . . . this is my lobstah tendah . . . call her the Yankee Doodle . . . she's an oldah boat . . . but she's as solid as a brick outhouse . . . Yessuh!"* "Harold . . . Harold Tuttle

. . . I live in Minneapolis . . . just out here on vacation. My wife's back in town looking at stuff . . . you know . . . gift shops." *"Ayuh . . . the misses wooks in one of them theyah stowahs . . . the Maine Goose . . . er . . . somthin like that."* Bill got down on one knee and began to scratch Walter's ears. *"What's his name?"* inquired Bill. "Well, his real name is Walter . . . but I think that's kind of uppity . . . I call him all sorts of things." Bill burst out in a belly laugh . . . *"Well Harold . . . I got to tell ya . . . Waltah heyah is the biggest poodle I evah did see!"* And with that he wrapped his long arms around Walter and gave him an affectionate hug. Walter responded with a lick to Bill's ear. As he straightened himself up Bill asked *"Whayah you stayin at?"* "Well . . . we haven't gotten there yet." answered Harold. "Got a friend out in Minneapolis, Jim Dinsmore . . . he's got a cabin just north of Camden Harbor . . ." *"Jimmy Dinsmowah. Why I've known Jimmy all my life! I spend a fayah bit'o time with his brothah Bernie up at the lobstah co-op in Belfast . . . Why yessuh . . . Jimmy Dinsmowah . . . ain't it a wicked small woold?"* As Harold and Walter started back toward the town, Bill yelled up from the deck of the Yankee Doodle . . . *"Hey, Harold . . . you thinkin of getting the Baby Titanic out on the watah? Just make showah the drain plugs in good n'tight . . . don't want the Coasties to have to tow ya in . . . Frankie . . . er . . . Commandah Sullivan was pretty ticked off at havin to tow that ole tub in last time . . . said that Jimmy would get towed by the salvage tug next time . . . and ole Dick Higgins . . . well . . . he'd chaage his own grandmuthah three hunded dollahs for a tow if her dingy was takin on watah!"*

Harold waved in acknowledgment as he walked up the hill back into town. Walter followed behind Harold only briefly pausing to lift his leg on an unfortunate umbrella temporarily parked outside a shop entrance. Harold caught the brief act of vandalism out of the corner of his eye. Turning around, Harold spoke sharply . . . "Walter!" His name would now be Walter . . . after all, any dog that would wiz on someone's personal belongings did not deserve terms of endearment! Frustrated at his canine's bad behavior, Harold grabbed the umbrella by the wooden handle and shook it briskly . . . effectively making the item pee-pee-free. He then pointed the sharp brass point menacingly at Walter and spoke with conviction . . . " Look here Mr. Tinklemeister!"

"Excuse me!" an excited voice behind him spoke . . . "What are you doing with my umbrella?" A red-faced woman in a tan dress suit and wide-brimmed hat stared at him intently. Realizing that this woman must certainly be a force to be reckoned with, Harold handed the desecrated object back to its owner and tried to force a smile. Harold felt flush with embarrassment as his smile wavered. He had tried this once before only to resemble the bumbling Charlie Brown...standing in front of his Peanuts friends with a pathetic wavy smile. Harold knew he was in a pickle. If he explained that his dog had inappropriately christened the umbrella . . . its owner could become even more furious and might demand restitution. An umbrella like that could be pricey.

Suddenly Harold came up with a brilliant escape plan. His mind desperately scoured the corners of his brain . . . frantically looking for any words of high school French that might not have been washed away by thirty years of neglect. "Pardon madame . . . " Harold began, "Je suis en vacances et je ne parle pas le langue anglais!" With that, he turned on his heel and began dragging Mr. Peebody down the street toward the SUV that would conveniently serve as a doggy penitentiary. When they had put no more than twenty feet behind them, the woman's voice called out above the traffic . . . "It's la langue anglaise . . . langue is feminine . . . so the nouns have to be in agreement...Jerk!"

Harold, red-faced and humiliated, walked briskly down the street seeking refuge inside the tall SUV with its dark-tinted windows. Harold hoped the angry and surprisingly francophone woman would not come his way. Scooting down in the driver's seat he looked more like a private detective on a stake-out than a carefree tourist on vacation.

Minutes later, Liz knocked on the side window. Hitting the unlock button, Harold sat up in his seat as Liz climbed in. Harold put the car in drive and pulled out cautiously into the one-way traffic through Rockland's waterfront shopping district. "Have fun?" asked Liz. "Oh ya . . . you?" inquired Harold. "Well, I walked from store to store...They have some lovely pottery back at one shop . . . I'll have to show you it sometime. It's handmade here in town by a nice lady I met. We talked quite a bit. Her name is Nancy . . . mmm . . . Nancy Stewart, I think? Her husband is John Stewart, the mayor of Rockland." "The mayor . . . cool . . . you're already hobnobbing with the upper crust!" said Harold as he adjusted the air conditioning. "I told her about our summer plans" continued Liz . . . " and they would like to have us join them for supper as soon as we get settled in." Harold smiled and nodded his head in approval.

Leave it to Liz to make friends and open new doors. "Oh . . . " Liz went on, "Nancy is really something. She not only makes beautiful pottery, but she teaches French at Rockland High School. Isn't that awesome?

Maybe you could try out your French on her?" Harold's throat went dry and he coughed violently. Grabbing the water bottle from his cup holder he unscrewed the top and took a long drink. Looking at him with concern, Liz whispered: "Poor man . . . I hope you aren't catching a cold or something!" Gripping the steering wheel and staring straight ahead Harold thought to himself . . . " Or something . . . mmm . . . that's it . . . or something!"

Chapter 4

Beware of Cheeks and Quahogs!

Heading north from Rockland, U.S. Route One rolls gently past Glen Cove and the white Dutch Colonial home of Down East magazine. "Look . . . Down East . . . I just love their magazine!" declared Liz holding up a worn copy as having the famed magazine in hand was proof they had her loyalty. The day after the *wicked good offah*," Debbie Dinsmore had shown up at her front door reeling under the weight of a stack of dog-eared Down East magazines, a tattered nautical chart of Penobscot Bay and a handwritten list of names and phone numbers. Each name was followed with comments like: "Sells good bait, white house before the red barn" or "Makes a good blueberry pie, watch out for her dog" and "Plays piano at church, husband delivers mail." None of the comments made much sense to Liz but she figured the information would prove valuable later.

The coffee-stained nautical chart was as incomprehensible to Liz and Harold as Swahili. Perhaps Bernie or one of the young "Coasties" stationed in Rockland Harbor would show them the basics. The magazines, on the other hand, proved to be a godsend. Liz scoured them eagerly for insight and information that could help make their time in Maine a cultural and geographic adventure. They provided Liz with advice on where to eat real "Chowdah" and a warning to avoid the canned stuff like the plague. Today an article unveiling a sinister plot to pawn off bogus seafood on unsuspecting tourists intrigued her. It opened her eyes to a world of culinary shenanigans to which she had been previously oblivious.

"Beware of!" the author wrote. "Authentic "Down East" chowder will most generally be made from Small Necked, Stone, or "Steamer" clams . . .

which have much more flavor than their giant, less tasty cousin the Quahog. In the fifties and sixties, Howard Johnson restaurants sold millions to unsuspecting tourists, a treat referred to as "Fried clam strips." Since Quahogs are four times the size of a regular New England clam, the copious mollusks were sliced, breaded, and deep-fried by the truckload. "Attention mes amis!" warned the food critic, "do not eat the canned chowder as it should, in truth, be labeled "Quahog Chowder." Liz was intrigued.

Never could she have imagined there was evil lurking in the dark side of "Tourist" seafood. . . . amazing . . . but she was even more amazed by the revelation that unscrupulous restaurants were selling "fresh Maine scallops" that were actually broiled or fried Cod cheeks! The writer claimed the walnut-sized piece of succulent white meat in the Cod's cheek that looked and tasted, for the world, like a scallop. Many years ago, Newfoundland fishermen working the Cod trawlers on the Grand Banks would enjoy feasts of pan-fried "Cheeks and tongues" after depositing thousands of filets into the freezer-hold of the ship. Tongues and cheeks were considered by the Newfies and New England fishermen to be a real treat. "Imagine that!" uttered Liz . . . "Did you know people try to pass off Cod cheeks as Scallops?" Harold, deep in a book on East Coast waterfowl looked over his reading glasses and replied with a quizzical "Huh?"

Back in their Eden Prairie home, coffee in hand, Liz would scour the stack of "Down East" magazines, making lists of places to go and things she and Harold "simply must see." Now Harold had turned right off of the highway and had meandered downhill into picturesque Rockport. Momentarily lifting her gaze from an article about birdhouses made entirely from scrap wood, wire, and car parts, a large blue and gold sign caught her attention: "Rockport Opera House."

This, proclaimed Jim and Debbie Dinsmore, was the culture capital of the Mid-coast Maine. "Yessuh" mused Jim . . . "Portland may have the Civic Center and the Merrill Auditorium . . . but it's got nothing on our little Opera House," Jim explained. "Oh sure . . . the Civic Center's fine for the big rock shows . . . and the Merrill Auditorium is nice for a full orchestra . . . but nothing comes close to the Rockport Opera House for class and intimacy."

Built in an era before sound and lights existed, the Opera house was designed so the many levels of balcony seats would all be close to the small wooden stage. Jim recounted how in seventy-two he had seen the great Danish pianist/comedian Victor Borge in person at the Opera House. He performed his zany comedy mixed with a piano mastery unlike Jim had ever witnessed before. When Borge fell off of his piano bench in jest, Jim laughed until the tears streamed down his face. The iconic Borge, the enormous black Steinway piano, and the stage seemed so close Jim felt he was Borge's private audience. "That is how the Opera House feels . . . like you are right there." He was sure Victor had made eye contact with him several times. After the show, the master jokster-virtuoso was congenial and personable, signing autographs and having his picture taken with his fans. Over Jim's office desk hangs a dog-eared black and white glossy of the Danish comedian bearing the words "To my friend Billy, all the best Victor." Jim had insisted that his name was Jim, not Billy to which he laughed, patted him on the head, and proclaimed "Nonsense! Tonight, I vill call you Billy."

"Over the years" Jim went on, "I've seen some big names there . . . James Taylor, Arlo Guthrie, Yo-Yo Ma, Carol King, and guitarist Leo Kottke. If you want to see real talent in an intimate setting," insisted Jim, "check out the Opera House. And that was exactly what Liz had in mind.

Coming into Camden, the traffic slowed to a crawl. "I wonder what the traffic is like here in July," mused Liz. "Not to worry," retorted Harold in a melancholic tone . . . "We will never be around here in July!" Harold took note of the wide variety of cars and studied their license plates: Massachusetts, Connecticut, Pennsylvania, Florida, Nebraska, Arizona, Ontario, Illinois, and even one SUV from Alaska. "Where are all the Mainers?" asked Harold. "Don't know," answered Liz softly, "Maybe they are all out of town?" After finding a parking spot by the town library Harold and Liz made their way down toward Camden Harbor. As they approached the crowded harbor area, the reason for the congestion became clear. Camden Harbor could only be referred to as "Postcard" perfect. Now they understood.

Camden was like something front page of an ocean vista calendar. Extending down from the restaurants and shopping area were wooden boardwalks running down to docks, their slips filled with graceful schooners, gleaming yachts, and sailing ships. There certainly was no comparing this sight to the working dock and lobster boats down at Rockland. This was where the rich and famous came to soak in the sun, eat fresh lobster, and play. On the walk in from the car, Harold had commented on the shiny black Bentley, a silver Aston Martin, and a long row of BMWs, Jaguars, Range Rovers, and Cadillac CTS wagons . . . noting they all were, as the locals say, "from away."

On the north edge of the bay, a steep hill rose from the water, boasting rows of terraced, multimillion-dollar homes and estates. It would surely take the camera gear of professional paparazzi to peek through the dense foliage getting a glimpse of the beautiful home . . . and one could only assume, of the beautiful people who resided there.

Harold and Liz found a table outside the Fungus Amungus Bistro . . . not twenty feet from a bobbing wooden sailboat. A tanned girl in her teens lay on a deck chair; iPad in hand, reading a glamour magazine. They ordered some soup and shared a Caesar salad and a Monte Cristo sandwich. The food was phenomenal . . . and so was the view. While they ate, they took in the vast array of boats coming and going from the harbor.

When the waitress returned, a cheerful, brown-eyed girl name Samantha, Hal cocked his thumb at the busy port and asked: "Where's everyone headed?" "Well," replied Samantha, "Penobscot Bay has lots of islands like Vinalhaven, North Haven, Isle au Haut, Deer Isle . . . oh gosh there must be a hundred islands. Some of these people live and work in Boston, New York, New Jersey . . . you know . . . executives and such, they come up here on the weekends to get away. You should see this place in the late fall . . . it empties out fast! Then you can actually park in town. How long you folks in town for?" "Well, we may here until November" answered Harold, "staying at a friend's cabin up the road a piece . . . say do you know where Mallard Pond Road is?"

Mallard Pond, as Samantha had explained, was just a big marsh overlooking the ocean at the foot of Mount Megunticook just south of Lincolnville Brach and the Vinalhaven ferry landing. It was, as she pointed out, very easy to drive by as the state had done a questionable job of trimming the tree limbs around the pale green road sign. Knowing how the locals felt about out-of-towners exploring every nook and cranny along the Maine coast, it was quite possible, she explained this was just another clever way of keeping tourists out of people's private drives.

Harold turned the SUV sharply onto Mallard Road and headed down a gravel road running through a dark pine forest. At the end of the road stood two yellow-painted telephone poles protruding about five feet above the ground. A rusty chain hung in a low ark across the road between the poles. In the middle dangled a thick brass padlock and a rusty sign proclaiming "Private." Stopping a few feet short of the chain, Harold smiled at Liz, extended his open palm, and announced, "The keys to the palace milady." Liz fumbled in her purse and triumphantly dropped the key ring labeled "#1 Mallard Pond Road" into his hand.

As they approached the brown log cabin, the sun had begun to set, casting a dark shadow over the woods, the cabin, the marsh, and the crashing ocean just beyond it. Looking at her watch Liz was surprised at how late it was. It had been a good day and now they were about to unpack Walter and all of their "gear" for the duration. Turning the key in the door, Harold made a gallant swoop of his hand and bowed as Liz stepped inside. Unable to wait for instructions, Walter darted between Harold's legs to begin his evaluation of their new digs. As he sprang forward Harold exclaimed sharply "Hey there Mr. Nosey-dog . . . slow down . . . we'll be here a while. Walter . . . "Mr. Nosey-dog" plowed ahead, pretending not to hear.

As Harold slammed the SUV's tailgate, a sharp crack of thunder echoed across the marshland followed by a thin blue streak of lightning. Harold felt raindrops on his back and shoulders. Opening the door, he dropped a large duffel bag on the floor and stomped his feet on a thick jute mat proclaiming: "Welcome . . . even if you're from away."

The rain beat on the metal roof producing a gentle roaring noise. Liz looked at Hal and appraised the temporary home: "Wow . . . this place is great . . . and that rain on the metal roof . . . it makes me want to curl up with a hot cocoa and a good book." "Well," replied Harold, "I know I packed a hot chocolate mix, and I did see a nice little bookstore in Camden . . . you will have to improvise tonight but tomorrow you can pick up a good book." Outside the lightening illuminated the craggy rocks and the white ocean spray. The lightning was followed by a deep bellow of thunder shaking the cabin. With a sly smile on her face, Liz pointed to a wicker armchair in the far corner. Sticking out from under the chair was a familiar long black curly nose and four black paws. "I am sure Mr. Scardypoodle will want to sleep near us tonight!" Harold added. As they prepared for bed, Liz discovered that Bernie's wife Betsy had made the bed up with soft flannel sheets and pillowcases. "Harold," said Liz as she unpacked the bags, "this Betsy lady is amazing! Did you check the fridge? She stocked it with fresh Milk, bread, eggs, butter, jam . . . looks like homemade blueberry, bacon, and orange juice!" Harold looked her way and mumbled in his best Homer Simpson voice... "Mmm . . . bacon!"

As Harold shaved, preened, and scrubbed himself squeaky clean, he marveled at the abundant hot water. Bernie must have turned on the water heater a day or two ago . . . why these good people have thought of everything!

Walking through the kitchen, he opened the refrigerator door and took in the provisions. Harold noticed one item Liz had failed to mention. On the inside door sat a bottle with a bright orange label that read "Moxie." A yellow post-it note read: "Harold, real Maine men drink Moxie . . . go for it! Bernie." Harold chuckled to himself but decided he was not quite ready for this adventure yet . . . so he shut the fridge and headed down the hallway.

Entering quietly into the bedroom, Harold found Liz dead to the world . . . wrapped in a hand-sewn cotton quilt with a seventy-pound poodle lying across her feet. Harold, disappointed but understanding, bent over and kissed her softly on the forehead. Harold shooed the big dog off the bed, turned off the nightstand lamp, and crawled into bed.

Listening to the rain as it beat on the roof, he soon understood how Liz, with all of her good intentions, could not have resisted the urge to fall asleep. Pondering this, Harold could no longer resist the Sandman's beckoning and in, but a brief moment had joined Liz in this wonderful slumber. In his fifty-six years, Harold had yet to experience this kind of sleep. In the weeks to follow, Harold and Liz would grow to cherish nights on Penobscot Bay with its rhythmic ocean waves crashing on the rocks, gentle breezes softly licking at the curtains and the rain drumming its beat out on the roof.

Somewhere deep in his dreams, Harold heard Liz calling his name. For a brief moment he couldn't discern if it was part of his dream . . . some bizarre reliving of his last day at McNeil and Durst . . . except everyone was dressed in party hats, blowing on noisemakers . . . and there amid the cacophony he heard the familiar voice of Liz . . . "Harold . . . Harold wake up . . . you've just got to see this!" Rising to the surface of his dream was like coming to the surface of a cool lake after having dived in. Breaking the surface of his consciousness, Harold realized he was in an unfamiliar place. He did not recognize the bed, the furniture, or the bedroom. Fumbling for his cell phone and rubbing his eyes, he was able to read "6:06 AM, Friday, September 3."

Six in the morning . . . what in the world was Liz up to at this hour? He found his jeans, and polo shirt and slipped on his Topsiders. At an outlet in "Freepot" Harold had succumbed to purchasing the tan boat shoes rationalizing "Well, hey . . . after all I'm in Maine now . . . and I could find myself hobnobbing on a yacht any day!"

Stepping into the hallway, Harold was greeted by Walter who insisted on licking whatever area of exposed skin he could access. Harold scratched the curly black ears for a moment and then proceeded to the living area. Liz met him with a smile on her face and a hot mug of Joe prepared especially the way Harold liked it...black, strong, and sweet. As he took the coffee, Liz said, "Sorry to get you up so early . . . but you've got to see this. She motioned like a traffic cop directing traffic. Her arms flailed indicating "Sir . . . right this way . . . sir...over here." "The sunrise here is absolutely awesome!" announced Liz. Harold had to agree. Looking out the wide living room window onto the coastline, the sun looked like a bright glowing tangerine rising gently up out of the water. Through its pinkish rays, one could make out a group of white seagulls circling above a red and white lobster boat as it bobbed up and down just beyond the menacing rocks of the shoreline. What a way to start the day! He was beginning to understand why Jim and Debbie Dinsmore missed this place. Suddenly he had a new compassion for his exiled pastor.

Chapter 5

A Blue Ribbon Welcome

Wiping shaving foam from his face he pondered "Maybe, just maybe I should grow a beard while I'm here . . . hmmm? I could use a more casual look." Hearing voices coming from the front of the house, he wondered who might have stopped by at such an early hour. Stepping into the kitchen, Harold was greeted with a cheerful *"Howdy theyah!"* from a tall lanky man dressed in khakis, Bean boots, a checkered cotton shirt, and a blue Boston Red Sox baseball cap. Beside him stood a small, thin woman with freckles, bright auburn hair, and a broad smile. The man stepped forward, extended a brown, weathered hand, and proclaimed *"Bernie . . . Bernie Dinsmowah . . . this heahs my wife Betsy."* Harold had met many Betsy's in his life . . . but this would be the first pronounced *"Betschy."* Pumping Bernie's muscular hand Harold warmly welcomed their first guests. Betsy had deposited a freshly baked blueberry pie on the countertop. Eyeing the golden lattice crust, Hal's stomach growled, and he wondered if Liz would allow him fresh Maine blueberry pie for breakfast.

"Thanks, Betsy . . . it looks incredible!" spoke Hal. It took some effort not to say "Betschy" and he wondered if they would be flattered or offended that a "flatlander" might try out the local dialect. Thinking it wiser not to attempt it without practice, Liz mercifully saved him by directing the topic of conversation to Jim and Debbie out in "Minnesoter." When Bernie talked, you could catch brief glimpses of Pastor Jim when, throwing all caution to the wind, would "Let'er rip" in full-blown Yankee. Bernie was a little older and a bit grayer . . . but you sure could tell they were brothers.

From there, they moved on to practical matters such as where to buy the cheapest gas, where to purchase groceries, where to find the post office, and what to do if the toilet backs up. *"Just don't use too much paypah . . . and if it backs up . . . theyahs a plungah that generally gets the job done."* From there the conversation went on to who the closest neighbors were. *"Most folk already know your heah . . . so don't be surprised if the townspeople greet you by name . . . you can thank Debbie for that. She sent e-mails to half the town . . . even attached your photo and asked all her friends to be nice to you . . . and she made sure to say you weren't "from away."*

Betsy gave Liz the grand tour of the closets and the idiosyncrasies of the stove, fridge, and washer and dryer. The men headed out to the shed where Bernie enlightened Harold on how to start the lawnmower, and weed trimmer and which gas can and oil mixture to use. Betsy came out with Liz and Walter in tow just as Bernie slapped Harold on the back, laughed, and announced, *"When you get good and settled in, we'll get the Baby Titanic stahted up. She's a wicked good little tub. Well Bub,"* proclaimed Bernie, *"I think you'll do just fine!"*

Harold thanked Bernie for the helpful information and followed it up with an invitation to "start the day off" with a hot cup of coffee and a fresh piece of Betsy's pie. *"Oh thanks,"* replied Bernie *"We've got a lot of errands to run . . . and I've got to get out and pull some traps before the mornin is gone."* With that he looked at his watch at exclaimed *"Well I'll be mollyhocked . . . it's almost eight thuty . . . betta get goin or I'll lose all the tide . . . set some traps in Gilkey's habah . . . and if I'm not cayaful . . . I could stove up the old boat on the rocks . . . so we'd bettah get a goin. By the way, Betsy won fust place with huh blueberry pie at the Union Fayah Blueberry Festival. It's wicked good . . . you won't be tastin bettah!"*

"Say . . . Harold, you'd be welcome to join us for chuch on Sunday mornin. We go to a real good chuch over in Appleton. It's not haad to find, just get on Route One out heah . . . go south to Camden and go west on Route 105 which is also called Hope Road . . . take that to Route 131 . . . that's also called Searsmont Road. You'll see the Chuch on the left. It's got a white sign out front that says "Appleton Community Chuch."

By now, Harold had deduced that "chuch" was the Yankee pronunciation for church. Whenever Harold or Liz were confused by the Maine dialect, they simply took out the "r's" and interjected them back where God never intended. This transformed "soda" or "pop" into "soder," "pizza" became "peetzer," "car" became "cah," and the city of "Bangor" was pronounced "Bangowah," actually adding an extra syllable. Feeling particularly confident of his new vocabulary skills, Harold nodded at Bernie smiled, and exclaimed *"Ayuh!"*

Being at the midpoint between Rockland and Belfast afforded the Tuttles choices as they could either head north to Belfast or south to Rockland to shop for groceries and life's necessities. If feeling adventurous or just missing city life, an hour north on U.S. Route One brings you to Bangor, Maine's second-largest city. Boasting a large, modern shopping mall, and a quaint riverfront area replete with eclectic gift shops, restaurants, and theaters, Bangor soon became the visitor's get-away of choice.

The Bangor Auditorium and Civic Center hosts world-class concerts and events. In the event of a medical crisis, Mid Maine Medical Center was located conveniently nearby, and Bangor has every stripe of fast food, automotive dealer, or retail service imaginable. The local "Bangor International Airport" is a major stopover point for both commercial and military aircraft. Reputed to have a runway long enough for even jumbo jets, it serves as the most northeasterly airport on the continental U.S.A. Should an aircraft have a fuel or a maintenance issue, Bangor International is the preferred option before heading out over the wide blue Atlantic.

Despite its rather demure reputation, Harold and Liz discovered Bangor was a "happening" town. However, today it would not be the big city so they headed twenty-four miles south to Rockland.

They purchased fuel and washed the car at the "Bells" Citgo, had lunch at the Pizza Hut then stopped for groceries at the large Walmart. Walking through the front doors, Liz commented on how this store looked like the one back in Minnesota. Harold reminded her that Walmart intentionally designed its stores to give shoppers a sense of familiarity. The one difference they discovered was the now familiar accent of the greeter who pushed a cart in their direction, smiled and said *"Hi, welcome to Wal-Maht."*

Their cart burdened with dog food, paper products, and groceries, Liz and Harold headed down the cosmetic aisle. Liz studied the vast assortment of shampoos, looking for her favorite brand as Harold focused his search on Old Spice deodorant. When he returned, he found Liz in deep conversation with a tall brown-haired woman. As he approached, Liz caught his eye and beaconing spoke: "Harold, I want you to meet Nancy Stewart!" Harold's heart stopped. This was the woman on whose umbrella Walter had emptied his bladder! To make matters worse, he had made an absolute horse's duff of himself by feigning being francophone. It had not worked, and she had publicly exposed his boobishness. "Boobishness" . . . that was it, mused Harold. It was indeed a real word. He had looked it up in Webster's, and it seemed the perfect description of his actions on that ill-fated day. What would she say . . . and how would he explain his folly to Liz?

The tall woman turned, smiled, and extended a long, elegant hand. "Enchanté!" Harold blushed and without missing a beat, the woman looked at Liz adding: "Oh we met outside my shop . . . the same day we met. Your dog took a special interest in my umbrella." Looking at Harold with a sly grin she went on, "Your husband speaks a little French . . . and I teach French . . . We should practice more sometime." Harold, at a loss for words, stammered in agreement grateful the details had been mercifully omitted.

"John and I are having a few friends over on Sunday evening" she continued, "It will be real casual. John loves to barbecue. Could you join us . . . say around seven?" Liz shot back an enthusiastic "Why we'd love to!" Reaching into her large pink and brown Coach purse, Nancy retrieved a small pastel blue business card. "Here, my address and cell phone are on the card. You can't miss the old place. See you then! With that, she was off, her sharp Italian boot heels resounding across the polished floor.

Heading north and "home," Liz approached the issue of appropriate party attire. Harold, generally compliant and good-natured, privately dreaded what could be a "Shackleton-sized expedition" required to find Liz just the right "look." As for himself, Harold considered a clean polo shirt, tan pants, and boat shoes to be appropriate for the upcoming soirée. "Really," scolded Liz, "you can be most frustrating. What's the Down East expression they use? An old curmudgeon?"

Turning the key in the door, Harold expected to be greeted with Walter's "glad you're home" bark. The house was surprisingly silent, causing Liz no small amount of concern. Turning on the kitchen light, she noticed blue paw prints crossing the kitchen floor, disappearing into the living room. On the floor lay a Pyrex pie plate, as clean as if it had just come out of the dishwasher. Behind her, Liz heard Harold dump several grocery bags on the countertop and exclaim with frustration "That pig! Walter ate the entire blueberry pie! At least I had one little taste of it!" "Can dogs eat blueberries?" inquired Liz anxiously. "I can't imagine why not," replied Harold calmly, "in Northern Minnesota, the bears eat them all summer." The blue paw print trail led the investigators to the guilty thief, a pot-bellied black poodle stretched out under a big wicker armchair. His brown eyes expressed guilt . . . but it was, no doubt, the guilt of having been discovered . . . not remorse from having consumed the blue-ribbon pie!

For the next few days, he would be called "Mr. Bluebeard" as his black muzzle bore a blue tinge from the blueberries. Liz wanted to scold him . . . but in truth, she and Harold had privately laughed about it. They treated him with mock anger, as they didn't want him to assume this was now acceptable doggy behavior. Harold pondered what it must have been like for the hungry dog, all alone . . . and that "wicked good" pie within muzzle reach. It was a temptation too great for poor Walter!

Chapter 6

"Welcome to Owah Chuch!"

Sunday morning broke on a cloudless bright blue sky. Opening a window, Liz hummed softly and took a deep breath of the crisp morning air. It was, she mused, an aromatic blend of salty ocean, wild meadow flowers, and pine needles. Harold stood on the deck; binoculars held tight to his eyes studying the cobalt blue of Penobscot Bay. Today it was exceptionally clear permitting him to see three islands: Islesboro to the north, North Haven to the south, and Vinalhaven just beyond Pulpit Harbor. He watched with interest as a silver-grey Coast Guard boat headed out to open water. Harold had been reading about the boats the Coast Guard used and this, from what he could see was the hardy, all-aluminum, forty-seven-foot patrol boat. Powered by twin turbo diesel v-eight engines, they were capable of running down Maritime law breakers night or day. Equipped with state-of-the-art electronics and enough firepower to reduce a fleeing vessel to flotsam, these rough-and-tumble boats were engineered to exceed ordinary sailor's standards of seaworthiness.

The "Forty-Seven" with its watertight hatches and windows could do a complete three-hundred-and-sixty-degree roll and faithfully land upright. On its conning tower, "Old Glory" flapped in the morning breeze as it churned up a massive white and green wake. Liz, equally intrigued, nudged Harold for the binoculars. "They aren't losing any time . . . I hope no one's in trouble!" she spoke in an anxious tone. "Well, if they are," Harold added, "those are just the guys to save their skin." Looking at her watch announced it was time to get ready for church.

Heading south, Harold and Liz noticed to their delight that Route One into Camden was relatively free of vehicles apart from a few locals busy about their errands. They turned right on the road labeled "Hope, Appleton, Union" and began to work their way west under the dark shadow of Mount Battie. They took in a group of tanned, sinewy cyclists pausing for a rest on the banks of Megunticook Lake, their multicolored speedos giving a festive appearance. Pulling into the already crowded parking lot of the Appleton Community Church Liz exclaimed: "Wow . . . popular place!" as she flipped down the visor to check her hair. "Ya," replied Harold . . . "must be a sale on or something?"

Entering the front door Harold and Liz were greeted with a boisterous and familiar *"Howdy theyah!"* Bernie Dinsmore had been assigned "greeter" duty and greeting he was. He pumped Harold's hand vigorously as if pumping water from a well. His broad smile and enthusiasm would no doubt convince any visitor these were indeed friendly people. "*Welcome to owah chuch!*" he bellowed. An older, quieter man in a dark blue suit and wire-rimmed glasses stepped toward them and extended his hand. "Good morning, I'm Pastor Osgood . . . please call me Randy." After a few moments of introduction, Pastor Osgood excused himself to prepare for the service. For the first time since entering the church, Liz had a moment to look around. The entryway was lined with dark pine wainscoting and the floors were of equally dark wood . . . perhaps solid maple or some other local hardwood. Liz was no expert, but she knew this building had to be at least a hundred and fifty years old . . . if not older. A quick glance at the wall outlets and switches told you this place had been built long before the invention of electricity.

The walls and the red Persian-style rugs gave off a dusty odor that evoked in Liz fond memories of her grandmother's house in northern Wisconsin. As a child, she had explored the vast attic and the treasures of its gigantic trunks, footlockers, boxes, and leather suitcases. She recalled opening a dust-covered trunk full of hats and shoes . . . it was exactly this smell. As she walked down a broad hallway, she noticed the distinct odor of coffee and the hubbub of animated conversation. At that very moment, Betsy Dinsmore exited the noisy hall with a little redheaded girl in tow.

"Liz!" exclaimed Betsy . . . "So glad you could make it." As the little girl ran off down the hall, Betsy gently led Liz toward the large hall. "We always have coffee and snacks before the service starts. Would you join me for a coffee?" Liz smiled and nodded and paused for a moment to notice Harold shaking a man's hand . . . already deep in conversation about . . . well, no doubt some "guy stuff" that men bantered about. Betsy introduced her to a half a dozen women and before long they were engrossed in a conversation about where to pick the late summer wildflowers and how best to dry and preserve them. Janet, a mail delivery person, even knew how to use certain flowers to make scented soap. Liz scrambled for a piece of scrap paper and began to quiz Janet on the step-by-step process of homemade soaps. About the time Janet finished her explanation, music began to emanate from the main sanctuary. "Time to go," whispered Harold, appearing from nowhere . . . "The service is starting."

Harold and Liz found a free spot on the front, right side of the old, wooden arched worship center. Liz was equally intrigued with the ancient arches and dark wooden pews. "Do you have any idea how old this place is?" whispered Liz. "As a matter of fact, I do . . . I'll show you something after the service."

The young, bearded man playing the guitar and leading worship seemed out of place on the archaic wood stage with the large velvet-covered chairs. The chairs were huge. They looked like something the Archbishop of Canterbury would plunk himself down on . . . but in this setting, with guitars, amplifiers, and cables running in every direction, the ornate chairs seemed a strange throwback to another era. Liz had discovered that Brad, the guitarist, and worship leader, was home from college in the Midwest and was in training to be a "Worship Pastor." Brad looked a bit out of place here too. Perhaps it was the "Weezer" T-shirt, the fluorescent yellow "WWJD" wristband, or the orange flip-flops . . . anyhow, the people loved him, and he certainly was a gifted musician. Accompanied by a pretty blond girl on drums, a chunky man in his fifties on bass, and a "blue-haired" lady at the piano who could have easily been his grandmother, the band was tight and on key. Harold, his preconceptions about stuffy country churches long behind him, found himself engaged in a raucous rendition of "Awesome God."

Dick Maurice, Appleton's fire chief and deacon, came up to give the announcements. Dick tapped the microphone several times making sure it was on before unfolding a crumpled bulletin containing the announcements. Dick reminded the congregation that the announcements were in their bulletin and invited them to read along. Opening her bulletin Liz began to read along while Dick continued. Dick read the announcement that, at 7 pm, Sunday night, there would be a young people's meeting at the Wallace's in Camden, a deacon's meeting at the church on Monday evening and the women's missionary prayer group would be meeting to finish the quilt they were sending to a young missionary couple in Peru.

Suddenly Liz poked Harold in the ribs and gave him the most impish expression. He responded with a muffled "What?" Liz gave no reply but simply gestured to wait . . . and placed her finger to her mouth and gave him the universal "Shhhh."

Dick continued to read. *"The chuch wants to remind everyone that flu season will be heah befowah you know it . . . and the Red Cross will be heah in the chuch hall on Thusday, Septembah twenty-second so come by and get your flu sh..."* Dick had stopped in mid-sentence . . . with good reason. The church secretary had overlooked a "doozie" of a typo in the bulletin. The phrase was supposed to have been "Come and get your flu shot." The "o" in the shot had been inadvertently replaced with an "i." It had gone unnoticed until this terrible, very public moment. As poor Dick stood stammering and red-faced, those following in the bulletin began to roar with laughter. A full five minutes of hilarious laughter ensued while Dick attempted to regain his composure. When finally able to speak, he quipped *"Well, I suppose you might get that too!"* and the crowd roared again.

When Pastor Osgood came to the pulpit, he broke the ice nicely with a comment on the importance of proofreading. The congregation affirmed his comment after which he launched out neatly into his sermon introduction. Harold was impressed with his professional demeanor and communication skills. His sermon was eloquent, yet practical. He had managed to explain a difficult and complex passage in rather simple, masterful terms.

After shaking hands with the pastor and a couple of deacons, Harold beckoned Liz to follow him. Leading her around a hallway to a back door, he pointed at an ancient, yellowed document in a massive frame. It was the original charter of Appleton Community Church. It began with the words "By the authority vested in the Province of Massachusetts Bay . . . " "Wait a minute . . . this is wrong," said Liz, "we're in Maine not Massachusetts." "Maine," explained Harold, "was part of Massachusetts until 1820 . . . and so was New Hampshire. It was called the "Province of Massachusetts Bay." You wondered how old this place was . . . well there you have it, April 6, 1816 . . . one hundred and ninety-three years old!"

On the drive home . . . or what they would call home for a while, the discussion was more about what the pastor had said than the terrible mess Dick Maurice had gotten himself into. In the communities surrounding

Appleton, the "Flu shot fiasco" would become infamous, inciting laughter for years to come.

Chapter 7

Harold's Shoes and Boobishness

Their first Sunday in Maine had been surprising. Appleton Community Church had been more of a vibrant, pleasurable experience than anticipated. They had been made to feel at home. As soon as they arrived at their temporary digs overlooking the deep blue of Penobscot Bay, Harold was assigned the task of taking Walter out for a tinkle and some exercise. At the same time, Liz jumped into making her homemade version of "Amatos Italian" sandwiches. At the "Shop and Save" they had picked up all of the ingredients including cold Cokes and Maine's own "Humpty Dumpty" potato chips. The long white rolls were cut with a v-notch to accommodate the ham, cheese, sliced green peppers, tomatoes, dill pickles, and black olives. The finishing touch was salt and pepper and a drizzle of olive oil. As they downed their lunch, Liz and Harold agreed that even though the ingredients seemed to be authentic . . . there was something different about the way they tasted at Amatos. Liz's creations were delicious, perhaps an eight or nine out of ten . . . but not quite as good as the sandwich shop. Someday they would discover their secret!

They coaxed Walter into the SUV and headed north to Belfast. At the bottom of Main Street, at the water's edge, they pulled into a spot and donned their hats and windbreakers. In 1720, General Samuel Waldo of Boston bought the Plantation of Passagassawakeag, named after the same-named river where it emptied into the Penobscot Bay. When Waldo died in 1759, his heirs sold the plantation to 35 Scottish-Irish proprietors from Londonderry, New Hampshire who renamed it Belfast after Belfast, Northern Ireland. The British military burned Belfast in 1779 and then held it for five days during the War of 1812. Following the war, the seaport was rebuilt and thrived. It developed into a shipbuilding center, producing hundreds of three, four, and five-masted schooners. The long pine logs used for boat construction were floated down the Penobscot River from Bangor, America's lumber capital during the later 19th century. To this day, Belfast boasts a vibrant shipyard and seafood dock.

Sitting on a long bench overlooking the water, Harold and Liz watched various ships and lobster tenders come and go while making sure their freshly purchased ice cream cones did not drip. The kind lady at the "Purple Cow" had offered Walter a small "doggy ice cream treat." He had consumed it in about twelve seconds . . . if that. He now lay at their feet licking the empty bowl as if it still contained a molecule or two of the treat. The seagulls cawed and circled overhead occasionally swooping down on passing boats, hoping to be tossed some morsel.

Liz buzzed in and out of shops and boutiques like a bee in a meadow. On the park bench by the bay, Harold had his nose buried deep in a paperback while Walter sat watching some bold seagulls that had landed near them. His wiry tail quivered with anticipation of taking his best pounce on the taunting birds. Harold tied the leash firmly to the bench. There would be no eating Mr. Seagull today. Walter had never actually tried to chomp down on a seagull before, but by state law, they were a protected species and Harold was in no mood to pay a four hundred and fifty dollar fine on behalf of a delinquent poodle.

They pulled back into the cabin drive as the afternoon sun was gently fading in the west. East Coast sunrises were spectacular, as the bright orange sun seemed to rise out of the blue ocean. Sunsets on the other hand were mediocre, the sun dropping over the edge of the White Mountains brought darkness as if somebody had turned off the lights. Having had a good dose of fresh air, walking, and sunshine the trio settled into their favorite snuggle spot. Walter was on his oversized doggy bed, on his back with four legs spread in as many directions, snoring. Liz, wrapped in a comforter, had been sipping chamomile tea when she gently laid down the mug and expired. Harold had taken a more sensible approach and had zonked out on the overstuffed leather recliner with one leg dangling over the armrest. They both joined Walter in snoring. Asleep in the arms of Morpheus the trio had lost all sense of time and reality. It was six-thirty when Liz jumped up from the sofa, looked at her wristwatch, and exclaimed "Oh my gosh! The Stewarts party!"

Harold drove madly, steering with his knee as he changed from his jeans and polo shirt into a dress shirt and dress slacks. Liz, ever modest, changed her clothing in spurts in between groups of oncoming traffic. Liz warned Harold to keep the SUV straight and steady. The last thing they needed to delay them further would be a friendly interview with the Maine State Troopers investigating a possible "Driving Under the Influence." Liz managed to do her makeup and hair in the Toyota's sun visor mirror. Harold was amazed at what this woman could pull off and still look great. They found a parking spot in front of the old captain's house and joined the last stragglers in signing the guest book on the table. Just as Liz was signing the book Nancy Stewart popped out of the fray with an exuberant "Liz . . . Harold . . . so glad you could make it! Grab a glass of bubbly and join me on the back deck."

They each grabbed a tall champagne flute and followed Nancy. The wide back deck was easily fifty feet long and perhaps thirty wide. Red cedar benches were built in the structure the entire length of the old white house. Every seat strategically offered a stunning view of the south end of Rockland harbor its lights twinkling in the distance.

Mayor John Stewart was in the middle of an animated tale involving his fishing buddies Governor King, Sheriff Anderson, and himself during a recent "Blue" fishing expedition out on Penobscot Bay. There must have been thirty guests standing in a large circle taking in the story when Nancy broke into John's story with "John . . . dear can you hold the story for just a second? I would like you to meet some new friends of ours. This is Harold and Liz Tuttle from Minneapolis." Harold and Liz nodded, shook hands with John, and began to greet their fellow guests.

As they stood there, an awkward silence slowly grew. The guests had begun, one by one, to look down at the new arrival's feet. Liz looked down and turned bright red. Harold was the last to look down and when he did, he wished he had not. He was wearing one brown, well-worn boat shoe and one brightly polished black loafer! Now it was his turn to blush. Harold broke the silence with a hardy "Oh . . . my shoes . . . well . . . I happen to have another pair just like them at home." To which the crowd roared approvingly. A couple of men slapped Harold on the back, laughed, and assured him the good people of Rockland, Maine were neither uppity nor unforgiving. Harold wandered off to talk "guy stuff" with a group of men while Nancy pulled Liz off into a group of women interested in sewing, quilting, crafts, and such.

What would have normally been a disaster, turned out to be a good icebreaker. On the way home Harold and Liz had a good laugh and had to admit that Harold's "boobishness" had worked in their favor by showing the Mainers that these Minnesota "flatlanders" were just ordinary people . . . even a bit goofy or disaster-prone. Almost every time they would meet one of their new friends on the streets of Rockland they would chat and interact in a warm and congenial manner however, they did notice the locals were discreetly checking out Harold's footwear!

Chapter 8

The Baby Titanic

Monday morning, Harold's cell phone buzzed. On the other end, a jovial Mainer inquired as to whether or not the Minnesotans had received their annual flu shot yet. The question was followed with a familiar guffaw announcing to the entire world that Bernie Dinsmore was in a particularly good mood. *"Listen heah chummy . . . it's a good day for us to get the Baby Titanic wet. What do you say? Just befowah Lincolnville . . . tuhn right on Pond Road . . . the yellah and red boathouse is owahs . . . see ya at one."*

Harold had anticipated some heavy lifting but when arriving at the boathouse he was amazed to find the Baby Titanic, a red and white Boston Whaler tri-hull, bobbing gently by the dock. Bernie was leaning over the back fiddling with the latches on a black outboard engine. Though a novice in all things marine, Harold knew an eighty-horsepower Mercury could be counted on to do two things well . . . transport them to their destination at an impressive rate of speed and drain their bank account when time to fill the large double tanks. He recalled Bud Peterson's definition of a boat: "A large hole in the water that one throws all of their money into!" "Oh well," thought Harold . . . it couldn't cost all that much . . . or could it?

Harold greeted Bernie and inquired as to how in the world he had managed to get the boat out of the boathouse and down the ramp by himself. Bernie smiled and tapped his head. *"Brains . . . chummy . . . that's how we do it. You got to be smaht . . . So we rigged up an electric winch . . . it pulls the boat up these planks on rollahs . . . and it just slides back down by gravity! Slick as a smelt. Nothin to it!"*

Liz found the appropriate life vests for everyone in the boathouse. She was not surprised when Bernie declined to wear his. Liz had been warned that many Maine lobstermen find flotation vests cumbersome and will not wear them. Falling overboard, many succumb when the icy Atlantic fills their boots and clothing making it impossible to swim. As the Maine coast is rocky with limited beaches, few ocean-working men venture into the water for a summer dip. As a result, many cannot swim, and they simply live with the risk.

Knowing she would probably not win this battle; she dropped the vest into the belly of the boat. Liz had read the Coast Guard required every occupant to at least have access to a personal flotation device, even if they did not wear it. While in Rockland, Liz had picked up some boating safety brochures and was learning all she could to stay safe . . . after all this was the Atlantic Ocean, not a small Minnesota lake. Out here, things could go south in a hurry, and she knew it . . . and now they were heading out to sea, and the enormity of the deep blue suddenly made them feel small. A twenty-one-foot boat may seem large in your garage or being towed behind the family SUV . . . but quickly feels puny and insignificant on the rolling ocean swell.

The Baby Titanic quickly planed out and settled into a chop-chop-chop as she hit the swells straight on. A fine spray rose from the bow as the boat skimmed the green waves. *"That theyuh's Grindel's Point"* yelled Bernie as he pointed off to the north. *"If you've got a the time, theyus an old friend I want you to meet out on Noth Haven."* Liz held her hat in the wind and nodded at Harold. Harold switched on his very best Maine accent and yelled into the wind *"Ayuh . . . Let'r rip!"* Bernie chortled at his new friend's sincere attempt and jammed the throttle wide open.

The twelve-mile run to North Haven was idyllic. Large Gulls screeched and circled close to lobster tenders that bobbed near enormous rocks and little inlets. Fellow boaters waved to their friend and colleague. Harold hung to the steering house rail and inquired "How in heck do you miss these rocks at night?" *"Well chummy . . . sometimes we don't!"* Bernie retorted with a wide grin. *"If I were you, I wouldn't come out here in fog or at night. My brothah stove this ole girl up onto a big one just off of Gilkey's Island! He was lucky . . . a little fibahglass repayuh and a tongue lashin from the Coasties . . . Like I said . . . he was lucky . . . don't push yoahs . . . "*

Bernie throttled back as he pulled into Pulpit Harbor, gently chugging toward a long wooden dock. A red-faced man with a red baseball cap and a salt and pepper beard grabbed the bow line as Bernie threw it to him and skillfully guided the boat within a foot of the dock. Harold admired the skill and wondered if he could ever learn to do this without wrecking something. Bernie flipped a couple of white rubber boat fenders over the side and snugged up the stern line to the mooring.

"Hey theyah Main-landah!" exclaimed the bearded man. *"Howdy to you islandah . . . good to see yoah still kickin!"* Bernie stepped off the boat and gave his host a generous bear hug. After brief introductions, the landing party followed their island host towards a tall grey-shingled house high on a ledge overlooking the harbor. As they walked up a long path, Bernie leaned towards Harold and Liz and spoke softly: *"If yoah evah in a pickle when out on the watah . . . Billy Simms is the man to know. He's saved my skin a couple of times . . . and he's a fust rate host. I can't tell ya how many folks he's had stay heah in his house when a stom came up sudden like . . . you'll love his wife. She's a real peach . . . and wait 'till you taste her wild Gooseberry taht!"*

Margaret Simms and two freckled blond girls stood on the wide porch step. *"Magrit"* was a tall, thin, strikingly handsome woman in her mid-forties. She looked like a Viking queen with long, flowing blond hair pulled back accentuating her long straight features. Her smile revealed white, quite perfect teeth and her blue eyes seemed to sparkle when she spoke. The two girls had been picking wild blueberries, a fact made evident by blue-stained fingers and lips, teeth and tongues. Liz wondered how many blueberries had made it into the yellow enamel pot. Margaret seemed not to care and gently caressed the girls as they moved in and out of her reach.

Margaret poured mugs of hot coffee as Billy began spinning a yarn about a young Jim Dinsmore, the Baby Titanic, the U.S. Coast Guard, and an unfortunately placed rock at the mouth of Gilkey's harbor. As he told the story, he became increasingly louder and could barely get the story out without doubling over in laughter. *"Yassuh . . . I tell ya"* Billy roared, *"Jim thought for sure the old tub would break right in half! But she nevah did . . . she's a tough old boat and when you fellers pulled in heah . . . I was mighty glad to see the old gurl can still cut'ah!"*

About then, Margaret brought out slices of fresh *"Fowah berry pie"* a Maine favorite made from four native berries: blueberries, blackberries, raspberries, and little wild strawberries. Margaret confessed softly that the crust had come from the Shop and Save in Rockland. Harold's stomach growled as she cut generous portions and slid them onto delicate white plates.

The afternoon had become a serendipitous foray into a way of life Harold and Liz had never been exposed to before. Talk of community life on the Maine coastal islands intrigued them. These islands, serviced by ferries seem to carry on an unhurried existence that mainlanders rarely enjoy. Several thousand Mainers inhabit the scores of islands dotting the coast from Portland to the Canadian border. These islands are even serviced by chaplains who, certified as boat captains, take care of the spiritual needs of the islanders including regular worship, the sacraments, weddings, baptisms, and even burials.

Harold and Liz felt as if they had been exposed to a unique culture that few discover. It was wonderful, serene, and completely different from anything they had ever experienced. On the way back, Bernie had both Harold and Liz get the feel of the Baby Titanic's mahogany and brass wheel, occasionally yelling directions over the roar of the outboard, the wind in their faces, and the rhythmic pounding of the waves against the sturdy hull.

Chapter 9

Falling in Love with the Down East

September on the Maine Coast turned the verdant green of late summer to vermillion and orange hues. The days turned into weeks as the trio explored the inlets, bays, and harbors that comprise the "Down East." The Maine coastline measures two hundred and twenty-eight miles from Kittery at the New Hampshire border north to the Canadian border at Machias. That figure doesn't give an accurate image of the enormity of Maine's coast. Should an adventurous soul have both the time and the stamina to follow the entire shoreline, it would not measure two hundred and twenty-eight miles, but rather an incredible three thousand four hundred and seventy-eight miles!

Down East Maine resembles a pair of gloves laid one above the other with fingers pointing to the right. It is on these "fingers" of land that Harold and Liz discovered postcard-perfect scenes of lighthouses, and quaint lobster boats making their way through the multi-colored trap buoys and jagged rocks where green ocean waves crashed and sprayed mist skyward in a thunderous glory. This was the breathtaking Maine the Dinsmore's had reminisced about, and for good reason!

Driving with the windows down provided them with generous wafts of a distinct salt-air aroma alerting them to the proximity of the mighty North Atlantic. They felt like ancient explorers discovering hidden treasures, discovering rare jewels . . . tiny inlets, and secluded bays hidden in the crook of a long, pine-covered granite arm far from the clicking of Japanese cameras or boisterous New Jersey tourists.

Beyond the fracas and cacophony of beautiful but tourist-crowded Boothbay Harbor, Liz and Harold discovered a quiet, seemingly yet-to-be-discovered inlet where Walter jumped with exuberance from rock to rock. Liz, binoculars raised, busily studied a large red sailboat making lazy circles around a small island while Harold, overcome with an unusual tranquility just sat and starred, transfixed by the blue majesty. Walter returned carrying a long-vacated crab shell in his wet muzzle, which he deposited on Liz's lap as a well-intentioned gift.

With their local explorations came strange-sounding Native American names. As European settlers established themselves on the Maine coast, they named several settlements after towns and villages in their homelands of England, Ireland, and Scotland. Examples of this are Portland, Bangor, and Belfast, however many bays, inlets, mountains, and rivers retained their Native Abnaki, Penobscot, or Passamaquoddy names. As Harold and Liz reconnoitered the land, they grew intrigued by the mixture of British and Aboriginal names: Rockland and Chickawaukie, Camden and Megunticook, Belfast and Quantabacook. This was Down East Maine, a unique blending of Native and European history.

The Gulf of Maine provides its inhabitants with a bounty of fresh seafood. The Gulf of Maine abounds with thirty-nine varieties of fish, not including lobsters, crabs, mussels, clams, or scallops. Over the centuries, fish has provided life to the peoples of Maine, and before the arrival of European settlers, the Native Indians were master fishermen. The name "Passamaquoddy" signifies "Those who pursue the Pollock," and the geographic region called Passamaquoddy means the "Pollock-plenty-place."

Harold, ever the history buff, reminded Liz over morning coffee, that when the Pilgrims landed at Plymouth Rock, they would have starved to death had not the Indians enlightened them in the many uses of Atlantic Cod. "History tells us," began Professor Tuttle, "that on March 16, 1621, an Abnaki Indian by the name of Samoset walked into the Plymouth settlement. The Pilgrims were frightened until he called out "Welcome" in English! He had learned English from the fishing boats that had sailed off the Northeast coast. Well anyway, after staying the night, Samoset left the next day and returned with another Indian named *Squanto* who spoke better English than Samoset. Squanto told the Pilgrims of his voyages across the ocean and his visits to England and Spain. It was in England where he had learned English."

"What about the fish?" interjected Liz. Harold held out his mug as Liz topped it off with fresh coffee. "Patience sweetheart . . . you see, without Squanto the Pilgrims would not have survived. He taught them how to tap the maple trees, he showed them which plants were poisonous and which had medicinal powers. He taught them how to plant the Indian corn by heaping the earth into low mounds over the precious seeds and then placing codfish in each mound. The fish fertilized the corn resulting in a life-saving harvest. That October, the Pilgrims found themselves with enough food to get them through the cruel New England winter." "OK, Mr. Smartypants . . . I'm impressed" said Liz in a mocking tone.

They discovered local diners of all shapes and sizes where local fish could be sampled. Liz soon became a fan of fresh fish *"chowdah"* served up at Young's Lobster Pound in Belfast. Good chowder, as Liz discovered would be creamy but not thick and pasty like the canned stuff. It would have a thin layer of melted butter on top of decadent cream, diced potatoes, perhaps a hint of caramelized onions, real bacon pieces, a little salt and pepper . . . all loaded with chunks of fresh Maine Cod, Pollock, Haddock, or Cusk. There was nothing quite as wonderful as enjoying a hot bowl of chowder at Young's while taking in the salt air and sun as local fishermen unloaded their catch.

The crisp fall weather had arrived, making boating a bone-chilling enterprise. Harold and Liz had worked hard at mastering basic seamanship skills and had become accustomed to exploring Penobscot Bay with the Baby Titanic. They had, so far, managed to stay out of trouble by watching for marker buoys, always staying within sight of land, and only venturing out when the weather permitted. The sun was high in the blue cloudless sky when they tied up at Young's Lobster Pound. Halfway through a creamy bowl of chowder, Liz looked at Harold and blurted out "You know what Harold Tuttle, I am beginning to love this place! I wish we could stay here . . . " Harold, chewing thoughtfully on a fried Haddock sandwich, stopped his masticating, smiled at her, and hummed a contented "Mmm. . . ."

Chapter 10

An Unexpected Call

The fall brought an exquisite orange glow to the Maine landscape. Children could be seen raking up huge mounds of golden and red Maple and Oak leaves which they would demolish with great leaps and dives. Mornings brought a light frost on the car windscreen and outings on Baby Titanic now demanded a solid jacket and a cap. For locals, a welcome change was the obvious reduction in the number of cars, bicycles, motorcycles, and RVs. Harold was the first to comment on this as parking in Camden became less difficult. "Listen to us," said Liz dropping a quarter in the meter, "we sound like locals!" referring to a comment Harold had just made about how glad he was to see the bulk of the tourists gone. There was no doubt that coastal Maine relied heavily on tourism to bolster the economy, however, it did become burdensome on the average Mainer who would be forced to leave for work thirty minutes early between June and September. Fall brought with it a different pace to life.

Customers pushing carts through the grocery store were now more likely to be locals, pausing to inquire about how the kids were settling back into school and if they liked their new teacher . . . how the bilge pump was holding up since the last repair . . . or if their son or daughter was doing OK away at University in Gorham or Orono. Some of the specialty stores and high-end restaurants were cutting back hours and when ordering lunch, one was more apt to be served by a local female adult as the young, bubbly teens had all gone back to school. They were experiencing for the first time, "normal" coastal life. It had a pace and flavor that appealed to them.

At the summer's end, an abundance of wild Maine blueberries had been for sale along Route One. Liz took full advantage of the bumper crop and Betsy Dinsmore and Willa Mae, the fire chief's wife from Appleton, had mentored her in the art of making all things blueberry. Now the apples were ripe on Appleton Ridge and her mentors were up to their armpits, helping Liz bake apple pies, and cook up apple preserves, apple butter, and applesauce. The thought of crisp Cortland apples made Harold's mouth water. He would miss them back in Minneapolis. Harold suggested he might have to rent a U-Haul trailer to get all of the preserves and such back to Minnesota.

The idea of returning to Eden Prairie stirred up mixed emotions. True, they missed their church family, their home of twenty years, and their friends . . . but they had begun to feel strangely at home, no longer feeling like tourists in town. Whether pumping gas, buying groceries, or picking up an item at *"Smitty's Hadware,"* they were greeted as locals, folk inquiring as to how the preserves were coming, how the Baby Titanic was holding up, and whether Walter had finally caught the skunk that had eluded him under the shed. Walter, currently being referred to as "Mr. Stinklesdog" was strictly verboten from riding in the family car until the aroma of skunk had dissipated. Smitty's bottle of "Skunk Rid" had done a good job . . . but you could still tell . . . especially when it rained.

They had become part of the fabric of Midcoast life, attending church lawn sales to benefit mission projects, a local Saturday night chowder cook-off in *"Nothpot"* and a David Mallett concert at the Rockport Opera House. "Kinda reminds me of Gordon Lightfoot don't you think?" Said Harold. "Ya . . . but you don't get to hear Lightfoot in Rockport." Answered Liz. "Ayuh" retorted Harold, grinning broadly.

Through the kitchen window Liz could see Harold pacing back and forth, cell phone pressed to his ear. A few minutes later Harold entered the kitchen with a grim expression on his face. "Liz," Harold began, "Pastor Osgood had a heart attack and was rushed to the ICU in Bangor. I guess he's going to be OK but only time will tell. That was Bernie, you won't believe why he called. The deacons had an emergency meeting last night and they want to know if I can speak next Sunday as Pastor Osgood will be recovering." Liz listened intently, her eyes moist. "I told them," continued Harold, "well I told them I am no pastor and there certainly must be somebody around better qualified than me. Well, Bernie and the deacons had a phone call with Pastor Jim and he said I was their man. He said that he had heard me address groups at Faith Community that were as big as or bigger than the church in Appleton." "What are you going to do?" interjected Liz. "Well, I told the Lord that I would do whatever He showed me I needed to do . . . so I guess I will have to say yes . . . and try not to say something stupid!" "Like switching to French when you don't know what to say?" said Liz with a chuckle. Harold glared at her and replied with a "Ha ha . . . funny!"

Chapter 11

The Confounded Lump

"Only five days to write my sermon." Said Harold. Having taught the adult "Pillars of Faith" class at Faith Community Church, Harold had the good fortune of his laptop's hard drive being loaded with teaching outlines. "Hmmm . . . what to use, what to use?" Harold pondered as he scrolled his mouse down the right hand of the screen. Wanting to share something appropriate, Harold looked through files labeled "Challenges for Today's Parents," "Becoming a Fully Devoted Follower" and "Living a Life That Counts," all interesting and stimulating topics . . . but nothing that shouted, "This is just what they need!" He scrolled down to a file labeled "Dealing with Life's Difficulties." There it was! Double-clicking the file opened a ten-page study on Mark chapter four where Jesus calmed the storm.

Pushing his reading glasses back up to the bridge of his nose, Harold began to read. "This is perfect!" he nearly shouted. It contained all the elements the good people at Appleton Community were facing fear, discouragement, uncertainty, a storm . . . and a God who seemed to be sleeping . . . seemingly uninterested. Of course, the study would show that the storms of life were normal . . . as was fear . . . and the disciples were not the first, nor the last believers who would stumble in their faith. At the end of their fear and struggles they would discover a Jesus who did indeed care and had the will and the ability to intercede. "This," thought Harold is appropriate. Bowing his head, he whispered "Thanks, Lord! Now, please show me what I need to say and how to say it."

That week went by like a blur, with Liz popping in and out of the cabin with bags of warm blueberry preserves and large quart jars labeled "Applesauce sweet," "Applesauce/Splenda" and "Applesauce no sweet." Betsy and Wilma Mae kept her hopping, and the results were nothing short of spectacular. Spreading some unsweetened applesauce on his hot buttered toast, Harold took a bite of what had to be the best fruit compote in the universe. "Cortland or Nutting Bumpus?" inquired Harold as the juice ran down his chin. "Neither," replied a red-cheeked Liz. "Macs." "I think the little Macintosh apples are a tad tart . . . but boy do they make great sauce!" "Mmm . . . you got that right Hun."

It was Friday and Harold worked on fine-tuning a sermon entitled "Does Jesus Care?" Every time he read through his outline and comments, Harold felt that confounded lump in his throat. He was no eloquent orator . . . and teaching an interactive class was sure a lot different than standing behind the pulpit, speaking to a group that would only listen and nod. These Mainers were not a demonstrative people and the best he could hope for might be the occasional *"Ayuh"* or *"Yessah."* By Saturday, Harold was himself experiencing his own private storm. He felt like his boat might sink . . . and did Jesus care? "Of course, he does!" thought Harold . . . but the confounded lump just kept coming back.

Walking Walter along the rocky shore, he was stirred by something Pastor Jim had said in a sermon about the young, fearful prophet Jeremiah: "God is not as interested in your abilities . . . or your inabilities . . . as he is your availability." Harold chewed on these words. He had heard his pastor say that at least a dozen times over the past years . . . but now was the time to face the giants in his own life. God, according to his wise pastor, was only really interested in obedience . . . being willing to do whatever God asked . . . and He would help Harold Tuttle to overcome the mighty lump in his throat. As he thought of the story of seventeen-year-old Jeremiah facing a nation of hard-hearted and rebellious people he recalled the Jeremiah text *"Do not say, 'I am too young.' You must go to everyone I send you to and say whatever I command you. 8 Do not be afraid of them, for I am with you and will rescue you," declares the Lord."*

As the waves crashed on the craggy, foaming coastline, Harold sensed that this was the answer he had been seeking. It was all about being obedient . . . not how clever or eloquent he would be. The revelation that it must never be about him . . . but always about God came as a relief. It was a moment of divine clarity knowing and understanding he would never find strength or ability in himself . . . but in the God that understood young Jeremiah and promised to both accompany and empower him. A feeling of confidence began to well up in Harold as he knelt and buried his tear-soaked face into Walter's warm neck. Suddenly the pebbled beach covered in flotsam, seaweed, and discarded shells had become sacred ground. In the years ahead, Harold would recall that ocean side yielding as the first steps toward a new calling to service and ministry.

Pulling into the church parking lot, Liz reached over and patted Harold's hand on the steering wheel. The engine had been turned off and Harold was just sitting staring through the windscreen. "You will do fine," said Liz reassuringly. *"Ayuh"* replied Harold with a grin as he opened the door and swung out.

Ninety minutes later, Harold and Liz stood shaking hands with the regulars. In an unusual display of affection, Bernie Dinsmore grabbed Harold by the shoulders and gave him a mighty shake. *"Yessuh . . . you did great! That was just what the doctah odad. I will run a copy of yoah suh-mon to Pastah Osgood. I am showah he will be as blessed by it as we all was. Betshy and I ahr gonna run up to the Bangowah hospital latah. We will say "hey" for you! And thanks again . . . you should be a pastah! You seem to have the gift."* "Right!" laughed Harold. "I was a nervous wreck. I guess God came through even when I was a mess." *"Daow!"* bellowed Bernie. *"That was great!"*

Driving home, Harold was overcome with spontaneity and swung the SUV left through the entrance gate of Camden Hills State Park. This time of year, the road winding up to the top of Mount Battie was open with no one collecting the summer toll fare. The drive to the top was smooth and surreal. During the summer season, few locals considered joining the long line of out-of-state tourists on the trek up the mountain. Today the leaves under their tires added a quiet swishing and bright red and yellow fall leaves could be seen doing acrobatics in their rearview mirror.

Climbing the rock lookout tower, Harold and Liz realized this was the first time they had ever found themselves alone to enjoy this coastal aerie. Almost a thousand feet below, the blue-green of Penobscot Bay was spectacular. "Look over there," whispered Liz pointing southeast, "you can see Camden. I love seeing the sailboats coming in and out of the harbor." *"Haabah Sweet Pea . . . it's pronounced Haabah."* Scowling back Liz cocked her head and uttered a perfect *"Ayuh!"* Harold bellowed with laughter, looking around to make sure they were still alone in their mountain perch. "You know what? We need to get back to Minnesota soon . . . but I sure am going to miss this place!"

Chapter 12

Back to Minne-Snowta

Interstate 94 from Tomah, Wisconsin to Minneapolis had been down to a crawl with dozens of spun-out cars littering the median strip. Studying the flashing blue and red emergency lights, Harold and Liz wondered about these stranded travelers, prisoners of their snowbound cars peering at the passing world through fogged-up windows.

"Isn't it interesting," Harold began, "How God uses circumstances to get your attention?" "Right," answered Liz. "Kind of like us." "Hmmmm" hummed Harold. "I wonder how these people's plans were changed today? You've got your plans and your to-do list and you're busy going here and there . . . and suddenly your car spins off the road and your day . . . or even your life is dramatically changed." "Or," countered Liz, "you go to Maine for a rest and suddenly you have new friends, a new life, you learn to laugh at tourists, drink weird 'soder' called Moxie, and the next thing you know your husband is wearing a shirt and tie, preaching . . . by golly . . . preaching . . . Harold B. Tuttle! Could you have ever conceived of such a thing?" Looking out his window Harold simply muttered "Whodathunkit?"

Its tires thickly coated with a brownish slush, the SUV squatted heavy under its load of suitcases and "Down East" loot as it nestled gently into its familiar stall. Walter immediately recognized his surroundings and hopping through the snowdrifts zealously marked his long-lost territory. The long drive from Wisconsin had provided Walter with ample ammunition and the local canine tinklers could quite literally give it their best shot . . . but these were his trees and let it be known to all errant whizzers . . . this was Walter's domain!

The house seemed to be just as they had left it. Swen and Sally Knutsen, a couple from the "Pillars" class, had been by to make sure the fridge was stocked, the heat was on, the mail piled on the table and the walkway shoveled. "Bless their souls," thought Liz as she slid into a freshly made bed. It was good to be home, and great to be back in their own bed.

Staring at the ceiling, Harold and Liz talked about the things they would accomplish tomorrow. It was, "good to be home." As they grew sleepy, they both sensed a tiny gnawing in their hearts they couldn't quite identify. Oh well, a good night's sleep and some fresh Starbucks "Verona" would bring everything into perspective. As he drifted off, Harold thought he could hear Penobscot Bay crashing and spraying the rocks outside. It was, he sadly realized, one of Eden Prairie's snowplows slamming great mounds of snow up against the end of their cul-de-sac. The sadness soon gave way to sweet dreams. After all, he was in the house he had dreamed of owning for years . . . snuggled next to what he considered to be the most wonderful wife a man could have. What more could he want?

The morning was bright and clear with a light dusting of snow making the pine trees in the yard look like a Currier and Ives print. As Harold thumbed his way through his freshly retrieved Star Tribune. Walter had managed to fetch it from the front walkway without doing too much damage to the bright yellow bag it came in. Harold was so engrossed in his morning reading that he barely noticed the kitchen phone singing its happy melody. "I'll get it," said Liz as she dropped a load of clothing on the big oak table. Harold focused deeper into the employment section of the paper. "Hmm," he mused. Thinking to himself, he pondered his future and wondered about what one does when you are suddenly unemployed at fifty-six. He thought back over the past thirty years in the Midwest's best ad agencies and PR firms. Could this old dog learn new tricks, or had he become a dinosaur?

Harold remembered the young guys the agency had hired before being sold . . . shaved heads, nose and ear studs, tattoos . . . all doing their creative design work on large-screen I-Macs. That was a fair description. He remembered smiling to himself when he noticed one of these "Millennials" was wearing bedroom slippers to work. Slippers at work, now that was even too much for Harold to accept but he knew the successful "Dot coms" had created a new, casual work environment. As he pondered that image, Liz appeared phone in hand, one hand covering the mouthpiece. "For you, it's "Pasta Jim.""

Harold was happy to hear the familiar voice of his dear friend and mentor. How he had missed the long conversations over Starbucks. "Love it . . . absolutely! Bucas after church. See you there." A glimmer in Harold's eyes told Liz everything. There were two things they both loved, Jim and Debbie Dinsmore and their favorite Italian restaurant. Harold had visions of chicken parmigiana, baked lasagna . . . and the garlic mashed potatoes were to die for. They could hardly wait! Good friends and good food, wow . . . could life get any better?

As the praise team led worship, Harold became acutely aware of the talent and fluidity these ministry professionals showed. Halfway through "How great is our God" Harold leaned over and whispered in Liz's ear "Not quite Appleton Community huh?" to which she responded by scribbling briefly in her worship folder. She passed it to Harold and winked. It said: "Yeah, but do they serve Betsy's triple-berry pie at coffee break?" Harold grinned. There he was thinking of food again.

As Pastor Jim spoke, Harold listened intently to a well-constructed sermon from the Gospel of John called "What do you do when Jesus says 'Follow me'?" It was the story of how Jesus stepped into the lives of his disciples, looked them in the eye, and basically said "OK . . . let's go . . . leave your nets behind...Follow me!" These disciples did the impossible. They followed and began new careers without knowing everything about the one they followed, without knowing their futures, and without promises made regarding their families, their homes, and their very lives.

Liz pondered the reality of what it must have been like for these men and their families to step into the unknown. She wondered what God might have ahead for them. For decades there had been a regular paycheck, a secure life, vacations, a few investments . . . and the blessing of a mortgage-free home. Down in her bones, Liz felt that God was going to open a new door for them, but she could not settle on what that could look like. On the drive to meet the Dinsmore's at Bucas, Liz expressed her musings to Harold. As it turns out, he had been equally troubled by the sermon, wondering just how this call to "Follow me" might play out in their lives.

The dinner with Pastor Jim and Debbie was superlative. It was so good to be with friends and enjoy a mouth-watering Italian feast. Bucas sure knew how to serve it up. They barely noticed the noise of other parties around them. Harold and Liz shared one story after another of their time in Maine. Now and then, Jim would roar with laughter and a hearty "*Well, yessuh!*" To egg him on, Harold would reply with an equally boisterous "*Ayuh.*"

When Harold told the story of how Walter had whizzed on Nancy Stewart's umbrella, Jim laughed until the tears ran down his face.

Leaning toward his tablemates, Jim whispered: "Bernie told me that you two fit in well both in the community and at church. I have to take my hat off to you both. Not everybody who heads east adapts to the quirkiness of coastal Maine. They say it's not for everybody . . . and I hear the people at Appleton appreciated you stepping in for Pastor Osgood." Harold smiled and replied in a confidential tone "Well to tell the truth I was scared to death! I sat in the car that morning and tried to get rid of the lump in my throat!" "Well, that," whispered Pastor Jim "is good news. When a man steps into the pulpit it is a sacred responsibility and should not be taken lightly! You were nervous because you wanted to do your very best. Being nervous is a good sign. Every time I step into the pulpit, I am a nervous wreck. Debbie will tell you." To which Debbie cooed a soft "Oh ya . . . a wreck!" "Well," responded Harold, "You sure had me fooled. Thanks for your transparency . . . I would never have guessed." Jim raised his tiny espresso cup with thumb and finger and offered up a soft "Here's to telling the truth!"

On the way home Liz looked at Harold and spoke "So what now Mr. Tuttle, advertising executive?" "Hmm" answered a contemplative Harold over the tick, tick, tick of the turn signals. "Tomorrow I will work on my CV. Scan my reference letters and begin to knock on doors. Let's see what doors the Lord might open . . . and let's see which ones He might close." Looking through the falling snow, Liz simply nodded her head in agreement. They entered the garage without speaking, as they both were deep in thought. Harold was still chewing on the morning sermon and wondering how they might respond should Jesus say, "Hey you . . . Harold and Liz . . . follow me."

Chapter 13

A Surprising Phone Message

Winter had settled upon Minnesota with a vengeance. Early December snowstorms were not uncommon in Eden Prairie, but the latest storm seemed to last forever. After three days inside, Liz was getting cabin fever. She was also getting weary of mopping the area around the kitchen door that led to the backyard. Every time Walter came in, the only part that remained black poodle was his paws, his tail, and the end of his nose. Snorting, he would shake his entire body, depositing a copious amount of snow on the kitchen floor. The rug by the door managed to soak up a bit of the melting deposit but Liz was beginning to tire of the many ins and outs of Mr. Snowball. In a way, she felt sorry for Walter as he was beginning to limp a bit upon returning to the warmth of the house. It wasn't hard to guess that the strange way the big dog walked was due to his paw pads beginning to freeze. Lying on his bed by the fireplace, Walter stretched out and gnawed on a rawhide treat, his favorite activity next to sleep itself.

Harold had ventured out to meet with an agency in the city. The drive-in had been slow, but he managed to find an underground parking spot near the IDS center where he had an appointment with the Randall McKinney group on the 26th floor. Four hours later, Harold coaxed the large SUV into the garage of 1501 Erickson Lane. He was glad to be home as it had been a tiresome ordeal. Although both his CV and reputation were impressive, he hated interviews. So many things could affect making the right first impression; for instance, being the first of four candidates being interviewed. By the time the last interview was over, they might have forgotten what you even looked like. It was, Harold considered, all in God's hands. Over the weeks, the interviews had gone well, but they always ended with a cordial "Thank you for coming in. We will be in touch when we have narrowed down the list of candidates."

Liz was just taking a mouth-watering roast out of the oven as Harold returned. Brown and crispy, covered with "Herbes de Provence," small potatoes and baby carrots surrounding it like soldiers entrenched around a besieged city. She placed the heavy dish on the oven top, turned, and met him with a warm smile.

Over supper, they discussed their day. The freshly baked yeast rolls seemed to scream: "Come on you know you can't resist some Maine Blueberry preserves on me!" Somehow both Harold and Liz heard the beckoning, so Liz made a pot of tea and returned to the table with a mason jar sporting a blue and white cloth over the lid. Recognizing it as some of the preserves Liz had made under the tutelage of Betsy and Willa Mae. He grinned and exclaimed "Ya . . . now there's a great idea!"

As he sipped the hot tea Harold began "You know, all of these jobs I have been working on. Well, they are OK . . . but I seem to be missing something. They are great jobs . . . but that is the problem. They are jobs . . . and I don't seem to have much passion about them. I could do the work . . . but it just lacks something that I can't define. Maybe they haven't called me back because my lack of "want to" is not overflowing. I know that I wouldn't hire me. Companies are looking for people with a "Fire in their belly . . . a passion." "Oh, I think you just need to get back in the groove," said Liz. "Groove huh?" Replied Harold as he spooned on a generous mountain of blueberry preserves. "Easy on the blueberries mister . . . who knows if we will ever get back to Maine to make more of that?" Harold made a sad face and spoke with his mouth full "We'd better, I can't live without this stuff!"

The next morning Harold rescued Liz from her cabin fever by taking her to lunch and a stroll in the Eden Prairie mall. It was good to stretch their legs and enjoy a brief although welcome reprieve from job hunting. Soon they both lost track of the world as they sipped coffee and thumbed through a serious pile of magazines at the Barnes and Noble coffee shop. Liz had a half dozen of her favorite cooking magazines, all of them determined to make this year's Christmas party a smashing success. Bon Appétit lured Liz in with a front cover photo and caption "Make this Christmas special with this easy-to-make German Marzipan-Stollen." Scanning the recipe, Liz promptly sat back and exclaimed: "You, know I bet I can make this!" To which Harold, lowered his reading glasses and muttered "Huh?

Make what?" Harold had been lost deep in an article on learning to tie your own trout flies. Liz looked down at his eclectic selection of magazines: Car and Driver, National Geographic, Popular Science, and Down East. "Down East" pondered Liz... "This can't be good. That will only get his brain spinning all night about Maine." Looking down, Harold read her thoughts and grinned. "*Ayuh* . . . there's a special article this month on Mount Katahdin. Someday we need to climb it. It's sixteen hundred feet high . . . and the trail is just about four miles to the summit. Can you believe it, there is a lake up there . . . I think it's called Mirror Lake?" Liz's expression was skeptical at best as she scrutinized the bright, glossy cover and retorted, "At our age . . . mountain climbing . . . are you kidding?" "Oh, come on . . . you're still a spring chicken!" replied Harold with a wide grin.

Walking in from the garage Harold and Liz were met by a conflicted Walter. He always greeted them as if they had been gone on a month-long excursion to some foreign land. Liz wondered if this was just Walter or did all dogs suffered from any sense of elapsed time. He wagged his stubby black tail so hard he looked like one of those battery-powered toy dogs stores put on the floor in to attract children. They wiggle and wiggle and turn in circles until the batteries die. Walter only wiggled for a short while as he was definitely interested in visiting the backyard . . . and soon if you please. The answering machine had three messages waiting.

The first message raised Harold's eyebrows and brought a grin to his face as it was from Sophia at the Randall McKinney Group letting him know they would like to schedule a follow-up interview for next Tuesday at 10 a.m. Harold scribbled on a yellow sticky note as the bubbly Sophia left her extension number, hoping to hear back from him soon. The next message was from Hugh and Barbara Kepke making sure they knew about the "Pillars" Christmas party coming up at their home. This was always a highlight. Hugh was an executive at Northwest Airlines and their home on Lake Minnetonka was, as Liz had commented, "To die for!" Their living room with its large fireplace and overstuffed leather chairs and sofas made it hard to get up after you had sat for a while. Liz's mind went to last Christmas sitting talking with friends, the crackling fire in the background, homemade eggnog in hand. She had wondered if anyone could ever create a more beautiful setting to while away an evening with good friends.

Liz reached out and grabbed the pad of yellow sticky notes that Harold had just laid down. As she scribbled the information she smiled at Harold and said wryly "Hmmm? A job interview, the world's greatest Christmas get-together . . . how could it get any better than this? They let the next message play through. They stood in the kitchen . . . speechless. Liz looked at Harold through tear-filled eyes. Harold stared upward as if looking at some invisible object on the ceiling. He too was overcome with emotion and wiping his eyes, he pulled out one of the kitchen chairs and sat down, limp from emotion. They could not have heard it correctly, so Liz pushed the "play" button again. They listened to the message again. Harold placed his arms around Liz as they wept together.

Chapter 14

A Little Pastoral Counsel, Please!

Liz opened the front door and greeted Pastor Jim and Debbie with an affectionate hug. "Honey, are you all right?" asked Debbie as she slid off her wool coat. "I think so" Liz replied with a tired smile. Harold came out from his office and warmly greeted his friends with a cheerful though subdued tone. "How about a coffee?" inquired Liz, which was met with a resounding "Yes please!" from her guests. As Liz poured coffee, Harold stood and said, well here's why I called you: We could use some level-headed advice. Liz and I have been on an emotional roller coaster and thought we should talk this through with our pastor . . . though I will tell you in advance that I fear I know what you will say. With that, Harold pushed the "play" button on the answering machine and Jim and Debbie smiled, immediately recognizing the familiar voice.

The message began in a thick down east drawl: *"Hey theyah Harold and Liz, this is Bernie Dinsmowah from Appleton, Maine. I am showah this message will take you by surprise . . . but don't you worrah, we've been prayin about this as a Chuch for several months . . . and we believe God has this all under control . . . so here I go: You might remembah that while you were down heah Pastor Osgood had a haht attack. Well, praise God he recovahed but his doctah has convinced him it is time to retiyah and move into a lovely little apatment his daughtah has in their home in Searspot. It is drop dead godjus as it looks out over the watah. He plans to preach now and again down at Lincolnville Beach as he is good friends with Pastah Swan, one of his old cronies. Anyhow, the Chuch bowahd has decided they would like to call you as our new pastah. They were quite impressed with your sermon last fall.*

They thought you were real and transparent. We are a simple people and like plain talk. Anyhow . . . you and Liz think about it and pray about it . . . and we will talk mowah. We can pay you what we paid Pastah Osgood . . . thuty thousand, some health insurance and you and Liz can live in the pahsonage. We just put a new fuhnace in and filled up the oil tank. We pay all the bills and take care of the fixin up. Oh . . . and if you accept there's a blueberry pie in it just for Waltah . . . I know how he loved the one we gave you!" at which Bernie roared with laughter. *"Anyhow . . . let us know . . . and we will be prayin."*

With a glint of something mischievous in his eyes, Pastor Jim grinned, lifted his coffee mug, winked at Harold, and exclaimed *"Ayuh!"* When the laughter had subsided, Jim took on a slightly more serious tone and began: "Hey guys, I think this is great. I know it is a surprise to you but I have been in conversation with the Appleton church for a while about this . . . so "mea culpa", yes I am partly to blame. They candidated several others and the committee was not impressed with anyone. Some others were too young and full of themselves while one insisted on selling the parsonage and building his own home.

Another wanted to make sure everybody in the church was homeschooling their children. Tony Robinson, who is on our board, is the principal of the middle school in Camden . . . well he just about had a bird! Tony is a godly man who prays privately for his students every day and he's very concerned about what happens when all of the Christian influence is removed from the public schools. So, they looked at several people . . . all good people . . . but they just didn't seem to connect with the people at Appleton Community.

I told them that, if they accepted, we would work out a plan to fill in some of your weak spots with some training. There's a great little Christian College in Bangor that specializes in helping "mature" students get ministry training in a part-time setting. You could drive up there in about a little more than an hour. The church will pay for the school bills and help cover your travel costs if you are interested. Anyhow . . . I have probably overloaded your brains with all of this. Let's meet at Starbucks next week and see where you are at in your thinking and how you are processing all of this!"

Long after Jim and Debbie's car had disappeared out of view into the crisp Minnesota night, they could still hear the crunching of the tires on the snow-covered lane. The sky was clear and coal black with the Northern Lights dancing a jig in the distant sky. "Wow . . . awesome," whispered Liz as her breath rose in a white cloud. Scanning the multicolored horizon, Harold reached down to find her hand. She squeezed him in response. "Are we crazy or what Mrs. Tuttle?" *"Ayuh"* responded Liz with a giggle.

Lying in bed, their minds would not wind down. Liz spoke in the darkness: "If we say yes . . . If . . . we will have to sell this house. The market's not great right now. Thank the Lord we are not upside down in it! At least we have some equity . . . " "Which," Harold replied "will need to be managed well as we have no idea how long we might be there . . . and we are back to that 'if' word. How about we sleep on it and we will face it tomorrow with a clear head." "Mmm . . . OK . . . remember what we studied in Matthew? How did that verse go? *So don't worry about tomorrow, for tomorrow will bring its own worries. Today's trouble is enough for today."*

Looking up in the darkness Harold grinned as he recalled how the Waltons had ended many episodes. Not able to resist Harold spoke loudly: "Good night, Mary Ellen" to which Liz returned a hearty "Good night, John Boy!" Beneath their thick-down comforter, they giggled like youngsters on a sleepover. Soon they were gone, both enjoying the reprieve from life's burdens that come with sweet slumber.

Chapter 15

A Night to "Remembah" with Bud and Dolly

The Delta DC9 shuddered and wiggled as it landed at Portland International Airport. Pulling his wheeled carry-on, Harold made his way to the National Car Rental desk and was pleased that, due to a shortage of small cars, they had upgraded him to a new Toyota Camry. "Hmm . . . sweet!" thought Harold as he guided the silky-smooth sedan onto Outer Congress Street. Soon he was headed north on Interstate 495, his mind spinning as he concocted a list of questions to ask the committee and worked on fine-tuning the answers he would give to their anticipated ones. The Appleton Pastoral Search Committee had given Harold the choice between landing in Portland and heading north . . . or landing in Bangor and heading south. Harold chose Portland as he had come this way before and felt comfortable in doing so. After returning Bernie Dinsmore's call, Harold and Liz began a series of phone calls to Bernie and the Search Committee. Comprised of six members, they thought it best to bring Harold out for a face-to-face meeting as there was far too much to discuss to use e-mails or conference calls. So here he was, back in Maine two months after they had departed. He was surprised, to say the least.

Heading up US Route One in Brunswick, his eye caught the bright red tomato-shaped sign announcing the location of an Amato's Italian sandwich shop. The very thought of their famous foot-long roll piled high with olives, pickles, veggies, sliced ham, and cheese seasoned with salt, pepper, and olive oil made his mouth water. Like the doomed ancient mariner, unable to resist the siren's call, Harold could not resist when he saw an Amatos!

He and Liz had made regular stops at several of these shops dotted up and down the Maine coastline and both would remark with insincerity, "Wow, I can't believe I ate the whole thing!" But they did . . . and with regularity. Sitting, thumbing through a dog-eared copy of the Portland Press Herald, Harold got into a rhythm . . . sandwich, wipe mouth . . . insert potato chip . . . sip Coke . . . repeat. He was suddenly overcome with melancholy as he remembered Liz at home, probably eating carrots with a small yogurt. Oh well . . . "I don't need to tell her I was here. No use in torturing the dear soul!" On the way out he grabbed a package labeled "Amato's Chocolate Whoopee Pie." He contemplated how he might consume this double-layer cake treat without having the vanilla cream filling ooze out onto his clothing. He paused, turned around, and grabbed a handful of paper towels. Smiling to himself he whispered, "Where there's a will, there a way!"

The GPS had him follow US Route One through Rockland, Rockport to Camden. Coming down the hill into Camden, Harold caught a brief glimpse of the harbor, which resembled a black and white photo with its winter snow and ice coating. He swung left on to Highway 105 and headed northwest. About five miles out, he bore right onto Highway 235 and as the instructions had noted, he began scanning the north side of the road for a small brown sign indicating the way to Moody Pond. The small, narrow road wound through the tall Maine pine trees woods as it followed the edge of the pond. Now and again, Harold could get brief glimpses of a wide, frozen expanse dotted with brightly painted fishing huts. The third mailbox had been painted to look like a yellow snowplow and bore the name "Munroe" in clean white letters. "This must be it," thought Harold. He double-checked his notepad which simply read "Bud and Dolly Munroe, retired D.O.T. worker, mid-seventies, large red farmhouse" Not a lot of information but it was a start.

As he stepped out into streams of sunlight coming down through the pine branches overhead, he was approached by an elderly German Shepherd who must have easily weighed over a hundred pounds. Harold's mind went back to when, as a boy, he had a Shepherd watchdog take a chunk out of his rear end. His father had warned him not to wander near the big dog sleeping on a chain. Memories came back to him of his father holding him in his tears. He could almost hear his father's voice "Now you understand why I told you not to go near that dog. That's a working dog . . . and he's just doing his job." Feelings of caution mixed with affection as he spoke kindly to the ancient canine. The dog looked slightly confused as it approached the visitor, wagged its tail, and took a sniff. Harold held out his hand and the old dog pushed it with its grey muzzle.

"Oh don't mind old Flash," hollered a voice from the back porch *"He's deaf and don't see too well. I'm Bud. Dolly's inside workin on suppah. Can I give ya a hand with yowah bags?"* Harold assured him he could manage and soon was ushered into a large living room. He was almost knocked over by an inferno of heat emanating from a black wood stove the size of a small car. "Wow, that's quite a stove you've got there!" commented Harold. Bud, reaching to hang up Harold's coat, replied with a toothy grin: *"Yessuh . . . I built that myself the last year I worked for the D.O.T. My boss told me I could use any scrap iron I could find. There was an old John Deere bulldozer that the DOT used in the sixties. Well suh . . . I cut that old baby up and made that beast of a wood stove. She'll crank out enough heat to blow ya right out o'the house!"* "Well, I can believe that!" replied Harold as he rubbed his hands together in front of the behemoth stove.

As the sun set, the winter darkness settled quickly over the coast like spilled ink on paper. Harold could hear and see snowmobiles buzzing across the frozen lake. In the ice huts lights glowed as fishermen stayed at their quest into the night. "Wow, it must be cold out there?" queried Harold. *"Daow . . . not too bad."* Replied Bud, *"Them tunkleheads stay out theyah all night! High tech . . . I'll tell ya . . . them shacks ah heated with beyah. Yessuh they drink beyah, lots of it . . . and that keeps 'em wahm! But by golly . . . if the Game Waden or the State troopas catch'em 'DUI' on those snow machines . . . well it ain't pretty . . . and they go to jail, loose theah geaah, the snowmachines. . . . everything. I'd say that makes for a mighty expensive lake trout! Yessuh"*

The evening meal was the kind you could write a book about. Dolly's homemade biscuits were huge, fluffy, and literally melted in your mouth. Dolly had opted for a traditional Maine meal of New England baked beans with pork and a touch of Maple syrup cooked in an oval cast iron pot which she sat in the center of the table, potato salad with dill and chopped eggs, another salad containing walnuts, dried cranberries, chopped chicken, mayonnaise and cut up red grapes. There was a slab of aged cheddar in the middle of the table and a tray of her famous "deviled eggs." The eggs were superlative, and Harold was informed Dolly had won a ribbon for them at the Union Fair last year. One bite and Harold rolled his eyes and exclaimed: "The best I have ever tasted!" And he meant it!

Dolly put on the teapot and reappeared carrying a massive tray of maple butter, Apple butter, and at least three kinds of fruit preserves. As she sat it on the table she added "Oh, I've got more biscuits hot out of the oven." Harold wondered how their hosts could stay relatively lean on this kind of diet . . . so he asked outright. The reply surprised him: *"Oh we heat with wood . . . and the wood comes off owah land. So, there's cuttin down the trees, draggin 'em ovah heah . . . got a little tracta fowah that . . . and then theyahs cutting up the logs, splittin 'em . . . pillin the wood . . . and Dolly heah carries in a good heap of it! That's the thing about wood . . . it gets ya wamed up bringin it in . . . and it wams ya up in the stove. Ayuh!"*

The dinner conversation had been informative, hilarious, and vigorous with the pitch of the conversations rising and falling with the storytelling and wry down-east commentary. Hal could not believe the depth of humor and wit in this unassuming couple. He had listened with rapture to the great Marshall Dodge's recordings of "Bert and I" stories and he and Liz had gone to the Bangor Auditorium to hear Noel Paul Stookey, Paul of the Peter, Paul, and Mary trio perform and share the stage with Maine humorist Tim Sample. Tim, pondered Harold, might not have a leg up on this real-to-life couple. The entire evening, they had kept him in stitches with their stories of understatement or exaggerations.

As the snowmobiles whined across the darkness of the frozen lake, Bud launched into a story about when old Charlie Swanson went through the thin spring ice just a short way off of Munroe's boat dock. According to Bud: *"Well suh . . . I heahd a mighty crack and looked out the window just as I saw old Chahlie disappear into the lake atop of his ski-doo. Well, I yelled for Dolly to call the fiyah station . . . and get out heah and fast. Wellsuh I took a flat aluminum john boat the kids play with and pushed it out onto the lake. When I got to the hole wheyah Chahlie had gone through . . . I looked down. Well, I'd say he was in about eight feet of cleah watah and I could see old Chahlie . . . sittin ontop of his skidoo . . . and he was a pullin and a pullin on the startah cohd . . . to no effect! I knew right away what I had to do or that fool would have drowned . . . so I got on my belly and cupped my hands to the water and yelled as loud as I could 'Choke it! Chahlie...she'll nevah staht like that . . . you got to choke it!"* With that, Bud and Dolly doubled over in fits of laughter. They had lured in the gullible "big city" preacher . . . set the hook and landed him before he had time to catch on! Embarrassed but amazed at their story-telling prowess, Harold had only to concede, admit they had the better of him, and join in the laughter.

Bud led Harold along a hallway lined with antique tintype photos of their ancestors. Bud explained, *"This has been owah family house since 1824. This is owah room heah on the right and you ahr right down the hall. Now you might considah leavin the bedroom dowah open as this old house ain't got no heat apaht from the wood stove in the livin room."* Harold was not keen on sleeping in a stranger's house with the bedroom door so when all of the "Good nights" had been said . . . he closed the door and unpacked his things. Coming back from the bathroom, Harold was frustrated that he had forgotten to pack his pajamas. Much to his dismay, he noticed a frost buildup on the ancient windowpane! He was quite sure he could see his breath.

The room was on the north side of the ancient farmhouse, and he could hear the bitter north wind howl and whistle as it assailed the red shingle siding. Harold did a brief inventory and calculated that he would dare not wear his clothing as it would leave him short for tomorrow's meeting and flight home. He would have to brave the cold night wearing only his socks, underwear, and t-shirt. As he slipped beneath the covers, he shivered and rubbed his limbs . . . hoping this would somehow warm the thick pile of quilts he had pulled high around his chin. As he lay in the darkness, he became aware that he had also forgotten his flashlight. As this old house was a "certain age," there were no wall switches anywhere. There was only one antique lamp by the bed, which was turned on and off with a key-like switch. Should Mother Nature call, he would simply have to feel his way down the hall and hope for the best.

Around midnight Harold was wakened by an unusual clicking noise. It took him several moments to figure out the sound was his own teeth chattering. He was cold . . . really cold. If he did not find a solution, he would never get any sleep and face tomorrow's meeting in a sleep-deprived haze . . . that is if they did not find his dead, stiff corpse beneath the covers first. He turned on the table lamp. Yes, it was official he could see his breath!

Harold scanned the room. Surely there must be some way of getting warm? And there it was, the answer had been staring him in the face. Harold got up and moved swiftly. He moved a chair towards the wall, picked up his suitcase and shoes, and put them on the chair. He then lifted the oak table beside the bed and tugged gently on the old, oval, braided rug. It was thick and heavy, but it would keep him warm. He dragged it over the bedcovers, turned off the light, and slid under the ponderous weight of the rug and covers. Soon he was sleeping.

Within an hour the quaking of his body recommenced. Now this was the second rude awakening of the night. He cursed himself for not bringing pajamas . . . or flashlight. There would only be one solution. He would have to open the bedroom door and let the wonderful, life-saving heat from the monster wood stove trickle in and fill his room. So, in the darkness, he slipped out from under the weight of his carpet and blanket sandwich and opened the door. As he did so, he could feel the warmth working its way down the hallway. "Sweet!" he muttered to himself as he slid back under the weight of his coverings. Soon he had returned to the dreamy slumber he craved.

In his dream, he had returned to the schoolyard of St. Peter Elementary School, St. Peter, Minnesota. His best friend Andy Erikson was planted on the other end of the see-saw, and they were having a jolly time of thrusting the see-saw up with their legs . . . and holding their legs out, landing like a frog as their partner went high in the autumn Minnesota sky. In Harold's mind, it was fall and the brightly colored leaves swirled around their heads as the wind caught them in a vortex. The old metal see-saw made a metallic, grating sound with every up and down. The sound kept on and on . . . even when Andy had disappeared from his dream, the see-saw continued. Hee . . . haw . . . Hee . . . haw . . . on it went. After about an hour of this irritating dream, he began to wonder if he was dreaming or was this real. He lifted his head out of the rug and bedding sandwich and listened. The noise he had been hearing was emanating from his host's bedroom. Bud and Dolly, snoring in syncopation were producing the very sound of the old St. Peter's see-saw.

Now Harold realized that this was the third time he had woken from his sleep and now awake, he became aware of an ever-growing need to visit the washroom. Disoriented, with no light to guide him, Harold stood, wavering like a man on stilts. He scolded himself for having three cups of Dolly's tea. Launching out into the darkness took the plunge with reckless abandon. Harold thought about the Polar Bear Club where questionably sane individuals chop holes in the ice and plunge into the sub-zero water just to prove it can be done. Now, stepping into the darkness he found himself standing directly on the most confusing surface. Its texture was that of a bristle brush except for its large size and slightly rounded shape. Under Harold's full weight, the hairy mass shuddered and rose up, bellowing like a cow...or perhaps was it a roar?

At that moment that terror overcame him, his hair standing on end as he muffled a scream rising in his throat. In the darkness, Harold attempted an Olympic broad jump off of the shrieking fur ball. His eyes were wide as hubcaps as he desperately searched the darkness. He hit the doorpost face first, stumbling backward onto what would later be identified as the bedside table. The lamp crashed to the ground and Harold found himself flat on his back in the middle of the floor. Surely, he would be ripped to shreds! Like Jezebel of old, there would be nothing left of him but little bits of his hands, feet, and skull. He shuddered at the thought. The wild beast was now running in frantic circles, bellowing like a wounded moose. Soon voices came from the hallway and the hallway lights came on revealing his plight. Furniture had been turned upside down, his clothing spread everywhere, a lamp lay decapitated on the floor, and down the hallway crashed a terrified aged German Shepherd bellowing like a mad bull. The hair on its back stood straight up...but then again, so was Harold's . . . and Bud's and Dolly's.

In the doorway appeared his host and hostess looking most troubled and perplexed. Suddenly aware of his state of undress, Harold pulled the rug over himself and stammered. In the hallway, Dolly chuckled to see Harold standing with the braided rug wrapped around him as Bud's voice boomed out *"Now don't you make no nevah mind about it! The old dog mustah slipped into yowah room when the dowah was opened. She's about stone deaf and don't see well ethah. She'll be all right . . . but what about you?* "Oh . . . I'll be fine." Replied a blushing Harold. Bud and Dolly continued to chuckle as they returned down the hallway. Harold imagined that the events of that night . . . the story of the terrified preacher wrapped in a rug would no doubt become part of Bud's extensive story repertoire. Harold had not heard the last of this episode.

A few minutes later, the house was quiet except for the see-saw which had begun to "hee-haw" again down the hall. Harold adjusted the warm comforter Dolly had brought him. As slumber once again seemed within reach, Harold smiled to himself and thought about what Liz would no doubt say to him: "Boobishness, Harold . . . you are the master of boobishness!"

Chapter 16

The Meeting

After a copious breakfast of Dolly's Maine blueberry pancakes and deer sausage patties, Harold bade his guest's farewell and headed into Camden. He managed to find a free spot in the Owl and Turtle's reading room where he would spend the next hour checking e-mails on his iPad and studying his resumé until he felt comfortable in handling most any question the Pastoral Search Committee might throw at him. He took a moment to greet the owner Dave and Sue Wallace. Dave and Sue attended the Appleton Community Church and seemed like a real asset. They had moved up from Boston in the mid-sixties and had settled into Camden where Dave taught high school English and literature while Sue worked as a nurse in Camden and then later at the new, state-of-the-art, Pen Bay Medical Center overlooking Glen Cove.

Harold was deep into his copy of the Portland Press Herald when a familiar voice roused him. *"Well yessuh! I heahd you waz in heah. Mighty good to see ya!"* Nearly spilling his coffee, Harold jumped up and hugged his old friend Bernie Dinsmore.

"Listen . . . Harold . . . we all talked it ovah . . . and if you don't mind . . . we . . . that is "the committee" decided to move owah meeting to the Helm restaurant. Say five thuty . . . we can meet till seven and you can drive down to Potland for ten or so. We booked you a room at the Holiday Inn right neyah the ayupot. In the mawnun you can return yowah cah . . . and get yowah flight back home." "Sounds like a plan!" replied Harold. Liz and I ate at the Helm last fall. The scallops were first-rate!"

The owner of the Helm ushered the group of ten into a quiet back room reserved for private parties. Not knowing how detailed the questions might be in this meeting, Harold was "loaded for bear." As it turned out, no one had any interest in grilling him about doctrinal minutia . . . whether Adam had a belly button, how many angels could fit on the head of a pin . . . or any of the foolishness he had heard about from some candidate "grill-ings." To his joy, the only thing grilled here was the fresh Atlantic salmon . . . if that was your choice. Several ordered fresh fish chowder, some had lightly battered whole clams, a couple had incredible-looking steaks and Harold ordered large sea scallops lightly crumbed, broiled in melted butter and lemon juice. This was no formal meeting . . . this was a party . . . a feast. If they were luring him in through camaraderie and delicious fresh Maine seafood . . . it was probably working.

Dick Maurice wiped his mouth and gave about a ninety-second speech to formally welcome what he hoped would be their next pastor. He opened the floor up to questions and as they ate, a few well-thought-out ones did come. They were mostly about Harold and Liz and whether or not they agreed about coming to Maine. Whether they would be all right in the an-cient parsonage. The committee did want this to work out. Sarah Cloutier commented that "word on the street" was that Liz had made some good friends and the ladies were looking forward to spending more time with her. They reiterated several times that they knew Harold had not formally accepted the position and were wondering if Harold had any questions that would help him make his decision. Harold asked a few questions about future plans and how the church was doing both spiritually and financially. The responses came freely from both sides of the table and all in all, Harold would describe the meeting to Liz as "Warm, encouraging, optimistic . . . they tried to make me feel wanted."

A light snow was falling as Harold said his goodbyes and assured them, He and Liz would spend some time talking . . . to each other, to God . . . and then he would let them know. The drive to Portland was slow but he man-aged to get behind a bright orange snowplow, which provided him with a nice smooth driving surface. His mind was spinning with the questions and answers . . . and with the sense of friendship he had felt. At Freeport, he pulled into the colossal L.L. Bean "Flagship store." He had promised to pick up Liz some of their thick flannel pajamas. Liz had turned red when Harold teased her about flannel jammies not being very sexy. Now his mind was spinning. He pondered his good fortune in being the undeserving recipient of a life partner who was, in his words: "Smart, godly and hot!" As he stepped out into the parking lot, he stretched and slid on his jacket. As he slammed the car door, an overhanging pine bough dumped fresh snow on his head, coating the inside of his glasses and sliding unmercifully down the back of his neck. Clenching his teeth, He muttered: "That'll clear my mind!" He worked the snow out of his hair and eyes as he trotted past the world's biggest "Bean boot" by the store's south side door. They were open . . . of course, they were . . . they never closed . . . ever.

Chapter 17

A Banner Sunday for the New "Pastah"

Sunday would be "a banner day" as it was the new minister's installation. Pastor Osgood had been invited to officiate the service followed by a "potluck" meal in the fellowship hall. The Camden Herald sent a reporter by the name of Steve Ellis to shoot some photos and write a piece for the religion section. The lady's trio had been working on a special number and the children had a song well-rehearsed and would make quite a stir. This was a song they had learned from "Sunshine Mountain" last summer's Vacation Bible School and as it was the third time, they had sung it publicly . . . it would no doubt bring a smile. Ruth Winters, the church secretary had produced an extra-large batch of bulletins and had spared no expense by producing them in color.

Harold felt conspicuous sitting in the oversized red velvet chair, which he referred to in private as the "archbishop's throne." From his vantage point, he could see all of the activities. He watched the pianist shuffle song sheets. Brad tuned his guitar silently twisting knobs while looking at a small box at his feet. For the first time, Harold took note that the bass player was doing the same. "Funny," thought Harold, "What you see from this perspective." In the back, he could see anxious toddlers being held back by their Sunday school teachers. Ushers were making sure the offering plates; guest cards and pencils were all in their proper places. Greeters were still shaking hands with those coming in and ushers were helping people find their places.

In the back left pew Harold could see a familiar face. It was Samantha. Today she looked different than the dreadful day on the breakwater. Sporting a red dress with her hair up in a knot on top of her head, she was wearing makeup and for the first time, Harold considered that she was, with a bit of fixing up, quite a pretty girl. The North Atlantic wind had nearly sucked the life out of her. Harold supposed that any female nearly hypothermic, ghostly white with running mascara would indeed look a bit like Alice Cooper "live" in concert. Harold wondered about the tears and why she was there on the breakwater. Anyhow he was glad to see her and today he knew she was both safe and in church. If she would give them half a chance, the kind people of Appleton Community Church would embrace her and make her feel welcome.

The program started at 10:30 sharp with a resounding call to worship by Marion Potter on the organ and Ed Carlson, the local funeral director on the piano. They had wonderfully managed to blend "Heaven Came Down," "I'm so happy" and "Wonderful Grace of Jesus." When they had finished the entire church was on its feet in response. Brad led the worship team in a series of three praise songs. "So far, so good," thought Harold . . . now if he could just avoid any major blunders! Dick Maurice now came up to make announcements and give some instructions regarding how the potluck meal would be served. Just remembering the last time Dick had made announcements triggered a smile on Harold's face. He was remembering the infamous "Flu shot" blunder. He covered his amusement by nodding affectionately at Liz. She smiled and nodded back. Then came the offering, the children's song and the lady's trio. Except for three-year-old Tommy trying to kiss four-year-old Sandra mid-song, the songs had gone off without a hitch. Next, Pastor Osgood came to the pulpit and did an outstanding job of saying the right things, not honoring Harold but rather managing to point everyone's thoughts and praises toward a kind and merciful God who, by His sovereign hand, had brought a new pastor and wife to the good people of Appleton Community Church. Now it was Harold's time to "respond." He began by thanking Pastor Osgood for his kind remarks and for being such a good shepherd to this flock. "You have made my path easier to walk . . . as over the years, you cared well for your flock, fed them exceedingly well and you have removed the rocks that I would have no doubt tripped over." A grateful Randy Osgood, arm around his bride of fifty years, nodded his head as a tear ran down his cheek.

Harold launched into his thoughts on lessons to be gleaned from John chapter ten where Jesus talks about being "The Good Shepherd." Although it was mid-winter in Maine, and no doubt in the twenties outside, inside the auditorium it was blazing hot. When the deacon in charge had arrived that morning, he had cranked up the furnace to a toasty seventy-five degrees. While the doors were being opened and closed as people arrived, the building never got to temperature. Now, with the doors closed and every seat occupied, the temperature had become downright tropical. As a drop of sweat ran down his back, Harold excused himself, slid off his coat adjusted his lapel mike, and took a drink. A dozen other constituents followed suit, glad their new pastor had decided to remove his coat, ushering in freedom for others who were equally over-heated. About halfway through the message, Harold sensed casualness in his address. He remembered when world-renowned Christian speaker Josh McDowell had spoken at their church in Minneapolis. McDowell had come down from the pulpit and half-standing, half-leaning spoke while supporting himself on the edge of the church's large communion table. Harold remembered it was a very "cool" thing to do as he was now on the same level as the people . . . not high above looking down from what some might consider a rather pompous elevated pulpit but on level with the people. Room dynamics can make a difference in a church setting.

As he spoke, Harold evaluated Appleton's communion table. It appeared massive, surely weighing as much as a small car. As he spoke, he took his bible in his hand and stepped down in front of the communion table. A murmur could be heard across the auditorium. As he leaned back, bible in hand, he continued his sermon. Harold wondered what new ground he might be breaking here in Appleton, Maine. They would be as impressed with Harold as he had been with a very cool Josh McDowell. "Surely," Harold mused, "they had called the coolest pastor ever." Now and again, he caught Liz's eye. She was not impressed and had a "This is going to bite you on the but" sort of look on her face. "Not to worry," thought Harold, "I have this under control." Harold made his three main points and then ended by quoting the words to an old hymn "Savior, like a shepherd lead us." He then invited the congregation to join him as he closed his message with a brief prayer. He had now laid his bible down on the large table and his hands were free. As he prayed, he took the opportunity to deftly tuck in the long-sleeved white shirt he was wearing. As he said "Amen", he turned around to pick up his bible when "Pastor Cool's" world came crashing down around him . . . literally.

Somehow when he had tucked in his shirttail, Harold had also tucked in the tablecloth from the Communion table. As he spun around in his confusion, the tablecloth emptied its contents onto the floor, into mid-air, and onto the unfortunate guests seated in the first two rows. Flowers, vases, and water became airborne landing on three elderly ladies who had sat close to the front. A large brass cross flipped end over end down the aisle while the eight offering plates, mercifully void of their contents crashed like cymbals, all rolling in different directions . . . mostly under occupied pews. In his confusion, he could not seem to figure out what was happening. Harold turned three hundred and sixty degrees several times before finally seeing the purple satin tablecloth following his movements. With his face red as a tomato, Harold reached around and pulled the tablecloth from the back of his trousers. As people sprang up to help pick up flowers, vases, cross, and plates, Brad came to the rescue and invited people to stand and join in a praise song he was already strumming loudly on his guitar. "Thank you Jesus for Brad!" thought Harold. He apologized to his newly baptized parishioners on the first row to which he received kind words of comfort during yet another moment of "Harold Tuttle boobishness."

As quickly as it had happened the disaster was over. Harold tucked in his shirt again, adjusted the lapel mike, and slid his mess of notes back into his bible. Brad dismissed the service and invited people to make their way to the Fellowship Hall and have lunch with Pastor Harold and Liz. As Harold scooped up Liz, she gave him a gentle peck on the cheek and whispered, "Say, don't you speak French?" "Ha ha . . . funny! You're going to milk this cow for all she's got aren't you?" To which Liz softly replied, "Moo . . . "

As they gathered around the tables Harold and Liz slipped into two places labeled Pastor and Mrs. Tuttle. As the crowds scraped chairs on the painted concrete floor and chatted, the recently retired Pastor Osgood broke the din. He was speaking into a microphone, making a serious attempt at quieting the rambunctious crowd. As the crowd hushed, he called everyone to silence and began to talk. *"It is a real pleasah to be heah today . . . and to help you welcome yowah new pastah. Now befowah we eat . . . we would like to offah Pastah Harold a very special napkin so he don't get any food or nuthin on his shirt."* To the howls of the entire Appleton Community Church congregation, the normally sedate Randy Osgood drew out the purple communion tablecloth and tucked it in Harold's shirt collar! The assembly roared with laughter. Harold also roared with laughter. Surely these had to be the most forgiving people on earth! He laughed loudly and looked sideways at Liz who was wiping tears of laughter from her eyes. She looked Harold straight in the eye and whispered, "Moo!" Once again, a generally composed Liz Tuttle doubled over in spasms of laughter. He knew . . . unfortunately she would not forget anything about this day and would savor the humor of his "boobishness" in the years to come. Moo indeed!

Chapter 18

A Mystery Solved

Hal held out his new clergy ID badge like Detective Joe Friday in the old Dragnet TV series. "Reverend Harold B. Tuttle, I'm here on official business." He growled aloud at an imaginary security guard blocking his access. Harold blushed Ferrari red as the couple in the car parked next to him raised their eyebrows in amusement. Trying to cover his boyish actions, he quickly spoke into his cell phone, a feeble attempt at throwing off the knowing couple.

The chubby woman at Penobscot Bay Medical Center's front desk was equally unimpressed with his credential badge, barely glancing up from her copy of Good Housekeeping. "Gladys Berry . . . oh ya . . . hmm . . . two-o-one . . . second floor." muttered the keeper of the fortress.

He found the witty matron of the Berry clan in grand spirits, sitting up and savoring a cup of applesauce with a plastic spoon. Seeing her new pastor, she announced with a grimace: *"This is a mighty powah excuse for applesauce. Now if ya like the real McCoy . . . I made fifty quats of Maine's very finest last fall. You and Liz will have to try some Pastah."* "Fair enough." He replied, "As soon as you get back to your big white house. *"Oh,"* chortled the animated senior, *"the doctah says I can go home next week! Can't wait to get back to the old place!"* replied Gladys with a twinkle in her eye. *"My sistah says that old place is too big for me. Maybe I ought to find someone to share it with. Six bedrooms ah just too much for an old geezah like me!*

They spent the next thirty minutes catching up on local news, what the boys were getting at the dock for lobster, plans to remodel the High School and the odds of Mayor Arthur being reelected. Harold loved spending time with Gladys. Her speech was peppered with coastal expressions and well-seasoned Maine humor. Spring was not far off, and she was lamenting what the old farm road would look like in late March. *"Mud season," she began "can be wicked if theyuhs lot's o snow. Why I remembah . . . 'twas in the spring of fifty-eight . . . the sun was up, and it was a nice wahm spring day when I happened to look down the road and I could see something coming up through the mud. I couldn't tell what it was but 'twas about the size of a cat . . . and it 'twere comin up the muddy road. Well, I took off across the front lawn to see just what it 'twas. As I got closer I could see the top of a hat. Well now I was just a surprised as can be when I saw 'twas a man, wearing a hat up to his shoulldahs in mud. I recognized the feller . . . 'twas my cousin Bustah Tompkins from Eastpot. Well now, I leaned ovah and yelled 'Bustah, what in tarnation ah you doin walking through that deep mud?' To which old Bustah yelled back 'Oh Gladys . . . I'm not walkin . . . I'm ah hosback!"*

As he walked toward his car, Harold chuckled at the subtleties of Maine humor. It seemed that when one of his parishioners began a story, there was just no way of telling whether or not the story contained even the smallest grain of truth. So once again, the clever Flatlander had taken the bait . . . hook, line, and sinker! "Imagine," mused the Reverend Tuttle, "being completely bamboozled by an innocent-looking spinster!" Well, it would either be Gladys who would reel him in, or Bud and Dolly Munroe with any one of a hundred stories they could spin. When together for meals with their new congregants, Harold was learning to watch the expressions of others. When they would wink and elbow the person next to them, it sent a clear message that they had heard this one before . . . a warning to be careful not to bite . . . or they would hook you and reel you in quicker than you could say *"Well now . . . let me tell you about old Bobby and the time he went Moose huntin with just a BB Gun."* Harold B. Tuttle would have to learn fact from fiction . . . a difficult task living amongst these clever Maine humorists!

Pulling into the parsonage drive, the late afternoon sun sparkled on the fast-melting snow. A snow-covered car was parked on the south side of the driveway. Harold could not quite tell if it was green or blue. Something about it seemed familiar. It would come to him. Long icicles hung from the eves of the ancient farmhouse. As he slammed the car door, one long icicle detached itself from the roof edge and made a "splosh" sound as it pierced the snow piled near the rear deck. "Glad that didn't land on me!" thought Hal as he opened the rear entry door. He hung his coat on a hook by the door and laid his leather bag on the kitchen counter. Out in the living room, Harold could barely make out the sounds of soft conversation. Normally he would announce his arrival with a bellowing "Liz . . . I'm home!" Today, he decided to take a calmer, quieter approach, which proved to be a wiser choice. As he poked his head into the living room doorframe, he noticed Liz had her arms around a younger woman who was softly sobbing into her shoulder. As she shuddered, Liz gently patted her pack and wept quietly with her.

Harold sat silently in the armchair facing the two women. Turning toward him the blubbering girl began to explain...or perhaps apologize. Harold looked her straight in the eye and softly whispered "Samantha . . . it's OK . . . you need to cry this out. Can I get you some water? I think we have Coke, Sprite . . . I will go see." The girl nodded and softly thanked him.

An hour later, Samantha had told her sad story of a broken heart, compromised values, and unrealistic expectations and now, at twenty-three, her hopes and dreams of college, a career, and a normal life had all been changed with the unborn child she carried in shame. To make matters worse, upon hearing the news, her mother exploded in anger and threw her out. Samantha was living temporarily with a high school girlfriend until she could figure out what to do. The baby's father was back at the University in Boston and would not answer her calls or e-mails. She was so confused. He said he had loved her . . . and her mother had reacted badly. Her father, divorced from her mother lived in Boston and had limited contact with her. Through her weeping Samantha mumbled something about her life being ruined. "No one will want me now." Liz, tears running down her cheeks, wrapped both arms around the heaving girl and simply held her without speaking.

As she slipped on her coat, Liz and Harold embraced her again. Harold struggled to encourage her without using platitudes or clichés, reminding her that God was ultimately in charge of conception . . . and even if this was not the best timing, God could use this for His good purposes. Earlier, Liz had read to her from the prophet Jeremiah . . . how God knew everything about the unborn child . . . and He had a plan for that little one's life. She spoke plainly to her about abortion not being the right solution . . . that like for little Jeremiah . . . God knew her child intimately before it was yet born. God would know his or her name . . . and would have a complete plan for that child's life.

Liz promised to share her story quietly and discreetly with mature women in their church who would no doubt rally to her aid and encourage her. "Remember," whispered Liz with conviction, "none of us are perfect, we all make mistakes, and our loving heavenly Father loves to redeem broken people and turn brokenness into blessing. Sam . . . God can do that with you. Do you believe it?" Tears streamed down Samantha's cheeks, and she buried her face into Liz's already damp shoulder.

As Sam started up her car and scraped a layer of ice off the windscreen, Harold and Liz stood quietly hand in hand. They did not speak until the red taillights disappeared into the dark night. Harold gave Liz a prolonged hug and quietly whispered: "Well at least we finally know the answer to the mystery of why she was on the rocks that day at the breakwater." "Yeah" answered Liz, "Waiting for the tide to sweep her away . . . to take her body and her pain into the deep blue ocean. Oh Lord I don't even want to think about what might have happened had we not taken that walk." "Don't go there!" Replied Harold. "That's God's territory."

Chapter 19

Mud Season in Appleton

Spring settled on midcoast Maine with little, if any, warning. The dappled snowbanks lining the streets quietly melted into rivulets winding through town. Verdant buds sprouted on an array of bushes and trees. It seemed to have happened overnight, taking the locals quite by surprise. Camden's fleet of pickup trucks and SUVs outfitted with snowplows seemed strangely out of place with the barest hint of winter snow lingering in the shadows.

Harold thought about Gladys Berry's hilarious tale of mud season in Maine and wondered how the old gal was getting along alone on her sizable farm. Doc Sullivan at Pen Bay Medical Center had cornered him in the hallway, expressing his concern about Gladys living alone in a behemoth estate. "The best thing Pastor Tuttle would be if you could find someone to give her a handout there. Her health is not bad . . . but there's a lot to do out on the old homestead. I'd be mighty grateful if you'd chew on that a bit." Harold assured him he would . . . and he was. Perhaps today would be a good day to check in on her. He looked down by the Toyota's gear selector and counted four dollars in quarters, just what he would need at Smitty's car wash after a trek down Gladys' muddy farm road.

Harold called Liz on his cell inviting her to take a jaunt out to Gladys Berry's. Liz was enthusiastic and would meet him at the mailbox in ten minutes. She hopped in, bearing a freshly baked banana-nut loaf wrapped up in foil. Inhaling the aroma Harold grinned and said: "I hope you made more than one of those!" "Indeed, I did Pastor Tuttle," answered Liz. "Actually, I made four and froze two!" Looking ahead Harold smiled and whispered: "I am a lucky man."

Gladys was in rare form and insisted on making a pot of tea to go with Liz's gift. Along with the tea, came fresh homemade butter from her nephew Scott and clover honey from her own hives. She was full of stories and humor that flowed from a thankful heart. She was grateful to be mobile and to be back on the farm. As the banana bread vanished from the cream-colored plate, she expressed concern about how she would manage the garden this summer . . . or the flowers, the lawn, the chickens, the cats, and a copious litany of other farm-related matters.

Slogging through the muddy ruts of the Berry homestead then onto the blacktop Liz was pensive. Harold knew Liz's mental gears were spinning . . . and he dared not ask for details. She would dump it all out in due time. Pushing for details would come to naught until Liz had formulated her ideas and balanced out all of the issues in her mind. As they drove toward Route One, Harold said softly: "I've got a craving for an Amatos Italian. How about you?" "Only if it comes with Salt and Vinegar chips and a big kosher pickle!" "Done!" replied a triumphant Harold as he swung the big Toyota south toward Rockland.

With a fine line of olive oil following the curve of her chin, Liz grinned impishly, laid down the massive sandwich, and wiped away the evidence of her indulgence. A handful of chips and a sour pickle later, Liz looked Harold square in the eyes and proclaimed: "I have a wonderful idea! You may think I am out of my gourd but hear me out.

Liz methodically unfolded the details of her plan. "Gladys needs help . . . and Samantha needs both companionship and a roof over her head. She needs a place to raise a baby . . . a place to call home. The Berry homestead would be perfect. If Gladys agrees, the men of the church can help take care of the things that Samantha cannot . . . say fixing a water pipe, tilling a garden, or mowing the lawn . . . I am sure we don't want her on that riding mower while she is in a motherly way!" Harold nodded emphatically and scratched his head. "Yes," he mused, as "out of the box" as her idea seemed . . . it made sense. What a great way to solve two or three problems in one fell swoop. It was genius. Now to find out what Gladys might think of the idea. Harold knew the truth . . . something this sensitive would be best left for Liz. She knew how to approach women . . . unlike Hal. She was still chiding him about his Sunday morning comment to Andrea Stevens. On a recent Sunday morning when Phil and Andrea entered the church, the ever-suave Pastor Tuttle warmly greeted them and then casually asked Andrea just when her baby was due. Andrea burst into tears and ran into the ladies' room. As the red-faced pastor stood perplexed and speechless, Phil explained that Andrea had recently joined "Curves" as she had put on some weight over the winter. To make matters worse she was quite self-conscious about her excess bulk. Yes, there was no doubt. When it came to tact, best to leave Liz in charge. She would have a cup of tea with Gladys early next week.

Chapter 20

Gladys Held Captive

A handful of sunny spring days combined with a brisk Atlantic breeze had done a *"humdinga"* of a job in drying up Knox County's muddy roads, making the trek up Gladys' long drive considerably smoother. Hal eased the SUV under the big oak tree remarking at the tree's magnificent spread. "I bet this tree was here before Maine was even given statehood." Liz looked over at him, smiled, and replied *"Ayuh."* They laughed together and stepped onto the thick grass underfoot.

On the broad, ornate porch Liz gently wrapped on the screen door's weathered frame. After a moment Liz pulled the door open, its long spring making a warbling noise. Sticking her head inside the door Liz hooted "Hello . . . Gladys . . . you there?" No reply. Giving Hal a concerned look she softly whispered: "I hope she's alright."

Together they searched the large creaking manor, amazed at the number of rooms this house held. Meeting at the top of the winding staircase Harold wondered aloud that the upstairs surely had to have at least ten rooms if not more. Liz, looking around spoke with a disconcerting air: "Yeah . . . all these rooms and no Gladys."

Having searched the house, they headed to a large garage and barn just north of the house. The garage yielded a riding Cub Cadet mower, a rusty old International pickup, and a seventies Dodge Dart in remarkable condition. The ancient Dodge was white with red seats and a push-button automatic transmission. "Would you look at this? I had one of these when I was a teenager. What a great car . . . I bet it's got a slant six motor . . . "

Harold's ranting about the antique car was suddenly cut short by a "shhh" from Liz. "Listen," she whispered. "Do you hear that?" Straining their ears, they could barely make out a faint "Hey . . . Hey . . . Hey" coming from behind the barn. Making their way around the building they discovered the source of the commotion. Behind the barn sat a brick red, two-door outhouse . . . a "privy" as it is referred to in Maine, occupied by a very loud and discontented octogenarian.

Harold spoke loudly "Gladys . . . you in there?" *"I am, and don't you come in!"* came the staccato reply from Gladys. Liz leaned into the door and shouted, "Gladys are you alright?"

What seemed like an eternity passed before Gladys volunteered any information regarding her situation. *"Last week,"* she quivered, *"I asked Dale Rigby to come over and varnish up these two seats for the season. I told him to lay it on thick . . . at least three coats so that it would hold up. Well, by golly that he did. He must have come by while I was in town with my sistah. Well, now, I came out heah . . . and now I'm stuck like a fly on sticky paper. I've been out heah two owahs . . . and I'm stuck fast."*

What happened next would generally be considered bizarre and outrageous . . . except in Coastal Maine . . . where legends and stories of this kind are more commonplace than some would admit.

Since no male species could be permitted into the ladies' side of the privy, the job of removing Gladys from the seat would fall to Liz. It soon became apparent no amount of tugging or prying would separate Gladys from the oak seat. There was only one way forward. Hal suggested Liz might unbolt the seat from the privy and bring Gladys out, seat and all. Normally in an emergency situation, a 9–1-1 call would be in order. It is always best to leave emergencies to the pros . . . but Gladys would have none of it.

After digging around the garage and tool shed, Harold amassed enough tools for Liz to proceed. After much grunting and groaning, banging knuckles, and working in a restricted space, Liz had the old girl free.

Liz emerged from the privy to inform Hal of a new twist. With a toilet seat firmly glued to her posterior, Gladys was unable to walk. She might hobble a few feet but no more.

Twenty minutes later, Gladys was kneeling, face down in the back of the SUV, bottom-up . . . mercifully covered from humiliation by a blue plastic tarp. Liz sat alongside her, helping her keep upright. At the wheel, Harold tried his very best to take corners gently and above all, avoid potholes. As he came onto Route One, he called the emergency room at Pen

Bay Medical Center and asked to speak to the nurse in charge. Soon nurse Spaulding was on the phone and to Harold's relief his friend Doc Sullivan would be waiting. Harold explained the situation and the normally composed Ann Spaulding struggled through hiccups of laughter, trying her best to maintain a professional composure. Between giggles, she assured Harold they would have acetone and paint thinner on hand and extricating the 80-year-old Gladys from her captor should pose no problem.

A rescue crew comprised of two orderlies and Nurse Spaulding met the SUV at the emergency entrance doors. They expertly slid Gladys onto a gurney face down . . . and seat up. They pulled the blue tarp over her strategically blocking the world from a sight from which they might never recover.

Halfway down the hallway, Doc Sullivan stopped the party and deftly lifted the tarp to take a peek. Harold, unable to contain himself any longer blurted out: "Doc, have you ever seen anything like that before?" Doc Sullivan winked and responded without hesitation:

"Well, as a matter of fact, I have . . . but I've never seen one framed quite like that before."

Having Gladys agree that it be good to have Samantha move in was like falling off a log. Recent circumstances had made her keenly aware that she needed help, and it would be good to have someone to share the big old house with. She had even determined to spend the funds needed to hook up all of the indoor plumbing and bring the Berry homestead into the twenty-first century. In short order, a new bathroom with a shower was built and as a joke, Samantha picked a shower curtain the same color as a blue tarp . . . " Just In case," she chuckled "it would ever be needed again." Gladys assured her there would be no need and mischievously winked at her.

In no time, the two became inseparable friends. It was not uncommon to see Samantha and Gladys bouncing around town in the old green Subaru, parked in front of the Dairy Queen, or picking up life's necessities at the Shop and Save in Rockland. They acted more and more like family every day. Liz had triumphed. Harold was ecstatic. All who knew the whole story had to smile, knowing that indeed "God works everything to the good of those who love Him."

Chapter 21

On the Bus with Gus

Hanging up the kitchen phone Hal looked at Liz with a puzzled expression. "That was Brad. He called to invite me to breakfast but he wouldn't explain where. He said I would never believe it and then burst out in laughter. He will pick me up at 7:30 tomorrow and a couple of the church men will meet us for a "feed" of the best blueberry pancakes on the planet . . . or at least that's what he claims. The strange part is he wouldn't tell me where."

"*Mornin Pastah!*" exclaimed Appleton's good-natured worship leader Brad Everett. "Mornin to you oh masterful worship leader!" retorted Hal, sliding across the pick-up's bench seat. Hal barely had his seat belt fastened when a mighty roar from the big V-8 pinned the occupants to their seats and propelled them up to speed in an impossibly short distance. "Wow. This thing flies!" yelled Harold over the whine of the big knobby tires. "*Yeah . . . but just between gas pumps! I'm happy when she gets ten miles per gallon . . . but I can't complain . . . she's paid for.*" Just about the time Hal was opening his mouth to comment, the big four-wheel drive hit a rise in the road nearly sending him airborne. Brad grinned mischievously and turned to his passenger who was now firmly fastened to the door handle. "*Sorry Pastah!*" Hal, growing accustomed to the rough Maine back roads simply smiled and came back with "Ayuh."

Where routes 131 and 17 intersect Brad pulled into a pine-shaded lot where a sizable row of cars was parked facing a bright red school bus. "*This is it,*" exclaimed Brad. "This is what?" queried Hal. "*This is it,*" replied Brad . . . "*The pride of Maine's breakfast restaurants par excellence! This my dear*

pastah is Gus' Breakfast Bus!" "You're kidding right?" shot back an incredu-
lous Harold Tuttle. Sliding out his door, Brad grinned. *"Come on . . . Gus
makes the best blueberry hotcakes in Maine . . . er well, that's my humble
opinion."* Grabbing the two-piece bus door, Brad deftly opened the way for
the pair to enter. Stepping up, Hal was suddenly taken back to the thousands of times he had stepped onto a school bus in rural Minnesota. He
was almost expecting to hear Gary Biggs yell "Hey Tuttle . . . what's with the
goofy mittens?" This time he was not greeted with mean-spirited jeers but
rather a cheerful chorus of *"Mornin Pastah!"* from Bernie Dinsmore, Dick
Maurice, Bud Munroe, Billy Simms and Maynard Jackson.

The front seat and controls remained intact to provide the bus with
mobility when needed. The middle had been transformed into an array of
tables and chairs while the back housed a carefully planned galley kitchen
where Gus Sanders, a local fireman/cook flipped pancakes on a cast iron
stove top while popping toast in and out of the toaster, turned, salted and
peppered eggs to perfection, fried bacon and sausages . . . all while sharing
amazing stories of life-saving acts of heroism interspersed with the tales of
the ridiculous. Firemen get to see it all, tragedy, triumph, and the unbeliev-
ably hilarious. To make this even more amazing, Gus handled all of this
while pouring giant mugs of hot Joe, passing plates loaded high through
an opening in the galley wall, and keeping track of orders on a paper pad.

After a brief exchange of introductions, Brad squeezed "Pastah T" into
a long table with this rowdy bunch Gus had named "The Appleton Breakfast Mafia." Gus was quite sure this motley crew was scaring away the upper
crust of society . . . but as they always left a good tip, he would continue to
tolerate their bad jokes, sarcasm, and great outbursts of laughter. Smiling,
Hal spoke: "Well, now I understand. Gus' Breakfast Bus . . . never heard
of it, but it sure is amazing! And the food looks phenomenal!" To which
an exuberant Gus roared, *"Oh it tastes bettah than it looks . . . and you can
thank the good lord for that!"* "Oh, I will, Gus . . . you can bet on it!"

Harold eyed an elderly couple sitting in a booth on the passenger side.
The woman was headfirst into a mouthwatering stack of blueberry hotcakes
while her husband sat reading the Bangor Daily, seemingly ignoring his
breakfast. Hal was perplexed and finally sauntered over out of curiosity.
The man put down his paper and warmly greeted Hal with *"Mornin."* Hal
stuck out his hand and introduced himself: "Hal, Hal Tuttle I'm the pastor
over at Appleton. Is there something wrong with your meal? I noticed you
didn't seem interested. *"Oh no suh . . . Gus makes the best hotcakes around*

these pahts . . . I'm just waitin fowah muthah to finish with the teeth." Hal turned bright red, mumbled an apology, and struggled to keep his composure as he returned to his table. Bernie winked and leaned over toward the red-faced clergy. *"We should'a told ya about them . . . sweet old couple . . . but sometimes he forgets his teeth. When that happens, he just has'ta wait!"*

Two hours later, the satisfied men lumbered down the exit steps onto the parking area. Hal knew there was more to this adventure than just breakfast with the boys. His new friends wanted to show the city-slicker pastor that good food could be found in places void of candles, crystal, or linen. With a worn driver's seat and a five-speed stick, this won the prize for the most unlikely breakfast nook he had ever seen. There was, however, no denying the blueberry pancakes were indeed in a class all their own. Whenever Hal or Liz had tried to make these at home, they were always dismayed at their horrible purple batter. Gus had shared the secret to his perfect pancakes: Freeze the blueberries then coat them with flour. Pour the batter on the grill then drop a generous handful into the pancake. That way the batter stayed white, while the juicy blueberries kept their purple goodness to themselves. Local butter and Maine maple syrup pushed them beyond good to superlative! They were in Harold's evaluation, simply the best he had ever tasted . . . and on a made-over school bus! He could hear Liz now: "You ate breakfast where? On a what? You're kidding? There was no kidding about this. Gus' Breakfast Bus . . . only in Maine!

Chapter 22

The Salt of the Earth

"You my friends," began the Reverend Tuttle, "are the saltiest people I have ever known. Not because some of you get a regular dose of seawater as you pull your traps, anchors, and lines . . . or when you get a face full of Penobscot Bay when the bay gets choppy, but because the Word of God tells us that as followers of Christ, we are indeed the salt of the earth. That applies to all of us . . . even us "flat landers" who don't get the opportunity to be on the water a whole lot. Matthew says this in chapter five, verse thirteen: 'You are the salt of the earth. But if the salt loses its saltiness, how can it be made salty again? It is no longer good for anything, except to be thrown out and trampled underfoot.'"

For about twenty minutes the Reverend unfolded what Jesus was trying to teach his followers about what it meant to be salt of the earth. As he spoke, he sensed a certain heightened interest on the part of his friends the "Appleton Breakfast Mafia." Perhaps spending time with their pastor over blueberry flapjacks had nurtured a desire in this group to pursue spiritual matters and Christian maturity. Hal suspected there could be something else on their minds.

As he wrapped things up, the early summer heat had gotten the best of fans that rotated back and forth on the platform and the building was beginning to swelter. The temperature had to be pushing high eighties or low nineties inside the auditorium. Hal could proceed no longer without a drink of water. As he paused and reached for the glass, a murmur could be heard rising up from the audience. As he raised the glass, the murmur grew louder. It was, admitted Hal, unfair to the congregation but the pastor was permitted a cold drink while the "heated" continued in their suffering but after all he was the pastor!

It was not until the Reverend Harold B. Tuttle took in a copious mouthful of the cool water that he realized the horrible truth. Knowing their pastor's text ahead of time, the deacons had acquired a bottle of Penobscot Bay's finest saltwater and had surreptitiously exchanged the well water for their salty brine. Their interest was not motivated by spiritual hunger or interest in garnering new truths from the sermon but was rather a pronounced interest in seeing what would happen when the over-heated preacher drank the seawater!

In one embarrassing motion, Harold attempted to dispose of the brine back into the glass. Unfortunately, the water would not be returned to its source as neatly as it had been drawn out. Harold coughed, spat, and wheezed as saltwater ran out his nose, down his neck, over the glass, and down his tie. The crowd having anticipated this moment, roared with laughter. In a moment, Dick Maurice was beside him bearing a towel and a glass of well water. Hal tasted the water cautiously provoking another volley of laughter from the congregation.

Harold cleaned up, regained his composure, straightened his tie, and studied his mischievous flock. Zeroing in on his breakfast buddies, who had decided to sit together for this "special" event, Hal began: "It has been my observation that pranks are something you do to those you care for . . . as a way of not letting them take themselves too seriously . . . even done perhaps for their good. Your prank this morning tells me that I am one of you . . . as we don't generally prank strangers. I am glad you consider Liz and me to be family. I will never read this passage again without recalling just how salty the water was . . . and how salty you all are.

May the Lord help us to always taste different from the world around us. Salt that has lost its saltiness is no good for anything . . . and the master throws it away. The spirit of family you have shared with me today is a blessing disguised as a prank . . . and we will try, in turn, to season those in need of good influence in the world we live in. As we go our way today, may the Good Lord help us to be mindful that we are a peculiar people . . . and are to bring light into darkness." In one brief instant, Harold had completely turned the prank on its head and had used it for good.

Brad led the closing chorus of "As the Deer" and they were dismissed. Many of the Appleton flock thanked Harold for being such a good sport and for bringing the truth of Matthew Five to life for them. The Appleton

Breakfast gang, feeling a tad bit guilty, were surprised recipients of generous hugs indicating forgiveness and affection.

As Harold started for the car, Liz slid her arm and whispered "Well, Pastor Tuttle, well done! You used a mess for your benefit today. You just barely avoided 'boobishness.'" I am proud of you. I bet that was the first time some of those men had ever received a hug from their pastor. You know how non-physical most Maine men are!

As Harold slid the keys into the Toyota's ignition, he could still taste the faintest hint of Penobscot Bay. "Hey . . . how about seafood at the Helm?" inquired Hal. "Yum" replied Liz.

As Harold and Liz followed the waitress to their table, Liz poked Hal in the ribs. Turning to Liz he could see at once what was on her mind. Sitting at a small table by the window was Brad accompanied by an attractive young lady. The raised menu concealed the precise identity of Brad's mystery guest but as they took their seats all became clear. As the menu came down, Brad and Samantha waved casually at Pastor Hal and Liz.

Sitting with her back toward the young couple, Liz grinned from ear to ear and whispered: "Well . . . would you look at that! I would never have guessed." "That my dear," replied Hal "is what you can file under 'God's mysterious working.' It is something you and I can never figure out. I am glad they are friends. They both could use a friend . . . and she will need a listening ear and a friend to help when that baby is born. On the way out, make sure we stop by and say hi. We don't want them to think we disapprove in any way. Frankly, I am tickled pink."

Chapter 23

A Mysterious Visitor

Returning from a morning hospital visit, Hal found Liz up to her elbows in pizza dough. Between spurts of information, Liz blew away a strand of blond hair that had fallen into her eyes. Flour coated both arms to the elbows as she kneaded the yeasty pile into something resembling a large smooth river rock. "Don't forget we have the youth group here tomorrow night, and I am making enough pizza for at least two dozen starving teens. Oh, yeah . . . the Dinsmore's and the Wallace's are also invited. I will need you to pick up some "Soder" and "fixins" at the Shop and Save in Rockland." Hal grinned and put on his best Coastal Maine accent: *"Ayuh . . . Soder and Pizzer . . . yessah"*

Looking up from her handiwork Liz interjected: "Oh, hey . . . I forgot to mention hon . . . a man came by to see if you were around. He didn't say who he was and said it was a 'personal matter.' I told him to check back, and he said he was in town for a couple of days and then he left. He was a serious kind of guy . . . a suit . . . like a cop or a detective. Anyhow I did see he had Massachusetts plates . . . a grey four-door . . . Ford I think." "Thanks . . . I think." Replied Harold as he pondered what all of this meant.

Two hours later, Hal pushed the cart through the aisles of the new Shop and Save, double checking his list: Mushrooms (Fresh not canned), green peppers, four pounds shredded mozzarella, two pounds shredded provolone, two pounds sliced pepperoni, one bag red onions, one clove garlic and the list went on and on. "Heavens!" thought Hal . . . it would have been easier to call in Pizza Hut, Dominoes, or Pappa Johns to the rescue . . . but he knew Liz would not hear of calling in "Industrial pizza." Although it

94

was Hal's preference, he kept his opinion to himself. He knew better than to get in Liz's way when she was on a creative streak!

On the way home, Hal stopped to fill up at the Circle K in Camden. As he pulled into the pumps, a grey sedan was just leaving. Mass plates . . . and Liz was right. It was a Ford Crown Vic . . . just like the police drive. Hmmm? What gives here?

As he drove, his mind spun. "I've paid my taxes. I am current in all of my finances. Has a crime been committed? I wonder if it's about somebody in our church?" After exhausting all of the possibilities he concluded that the mystery man would explain everything . . . in due time. The wait, however, was killing him! In the meantime, he had a trunk load of pizza "fixins" to deliver. Besides, he had to prepare a few thoughts to share with the youth group. Sitting down at his home office study he tried to gather his thoughts: "OK Tuttle, remember what it was like to be fifteen . . . so make it short, funny if you can . . . transparent is an absolute . . . and applicable. Don't be a boring, long-winded cur . . . what had Liz called him? A Curmudgeon?" Surely, he was far cooler than that?

Thursday morning was a quiet one in the church office. Ruth Winters, the church secretary had the bulletin printed, the sermon PowerPoint presentation put together and the weekly announcements, banking, and all major administrative details were under control. She was off to the post office to take care of a women's ministry mailing. Brad was off today as by Wednesday, he had his music all chosen, the words plugged into Ruth's PowerPoint, the chord charts and lyrics printed, and the worship team would rehearse that evening. The phones were set on "answer" and no one would interrupt the pastor as he worked on the next series of sermons. Apart from a fat groundhog intent on digging up the flowers by the church sign, Hal was alone on the church property. He walked down to the kitchen and brewed a pot of Folgers the way he liked it, double strong. "Mmmm," thought Hal as he sipped the dark nutty brew. "Just like Starbucks . . . and it didn't cost me $5 a cup!"

At his desk, he clicked the icon for "iTunes" and listened as Phil Keaggy amazed him one more time with incredible guitar licks on "Your love broke through." Thirty years ago, Hal and Liz had seen Phil in concert in Minneapolis and three decades later this song still raised goose bumps on his arms! Lost in a brief moment of playing "air guitar," Hal was brought back to earth by a sharp wrapping on the office entrance door. Turning down the music, Hal peered through his open doorway and caught a glimpse of a tall, attractive man pacing back and forth on the porch. Walking toward the door, Hal could see a grey Ford sedan parked in the visitor parking. Finally, the mysterious stranger had tracked him down. Hal sensed a certain relief in finally getting to the bottom of this.

Arriving home, Hal was greeted by a very happy Walter, his giant black tail beating a "dum, dum, dum" on the aluminum door. Pulling off his cap and tossing it onto a metal hook by the door, Harold's senses were kicked into high gear as he smelled Liz's wonderful pizzas baking. "Tuttle" he quietly whispered, "your sermonette will never hold a candle to the impact of these pizzas on the young people! Oh well . . . onward and upward!"

"Hon!" shouted Harold. "I'm not deaf!" spoke Liz as she stood up from checking her oven. "How was your day?" "Hmmm OK, the mysterious man from Massachusetts appeared. Nice fellow actually. He's not the IRS . . . or a cop or anything like that. He works for an insurance company . . . that's why the big sedan. It's his company wheels. But get this . . . he is Samantha's dad, John . . . John Gifford. He heard through a friend about Samantha's getting kicked out of her mom's . . . and about her being pregnant and it has been eating him up. He didn't have a clue how to contact her and Sam's mom won't talk to him . . . so he phoned around and someone in town said I could probably connect them.

After explaining his story, he asked if I might call Samantha and see if she would be willing to meet with him for a coffee or something. So, he stepped out of my office while I called Samantha. Well . . . poor kid . . . she bawled like a baby. When she had regained her composure, she said she would meet him at Bailey's Café in Camden at seven this evening. He gave me a bear hug nearly lifting me off the ground and then he was off in a cloud of dust."

Realizing that he had been talking non-stop he walked closer to Liz by the stove. She stood speechless. Tears ran down her cheeks as she hoarsely whispered: "This is what I have been asking God for. This is awesome!"

Chapter 24

An Iconic Surprise in Blue Hill

The early morning sky was a soft pink against the cobalt blue of Penobscot Bay. It was mid-June and the brisk morning air called for a light windbreaker as the Baby Titanic slapped the waves and headed northwest around Cape Rosier. Bernie and Betsy Dinsmore had promised to treat them to lunch at Sally's Restaurant at South Blue Hill. With the big Merc outboard howling, the Boston Whaler planned out, just touching the top of the swells. At the rate they were traveling, it would take them about an hour to cover the thirty miles of water to South Blue Hill. The same trip by car would add twenty miles and another half hour. From Lincolnville, they could cut between Eggemoggin Reach and Herricks, then head east by southeast between Deer Isle and Brooklin, then head north to South Blue Hill.

It was a spectacular day for a boat trip. Earlier, Bernie had made a phone call and said there was an old friend he wanted him to meet over lunch. It was late morning when the Baby Titanic pulled into Sand Point Marina. A lanky red-headed boy filled the fuel tank while Bernie and Hal combined their wad of eight, twenty-dollar bills. Lunch would be cheap . . . filling a boat, well, that was a different thing. They had agreed to split the gas. When all was said and done, a three-hour boat ride was a good deal at $20 per head . . . or so Hal reasoned.

Sallys was an unpretentious white clapboard house that smacked of Coastal Maine history. Among old, faded clippings from the Bangor Daily were signed photos of President Franklin D. Roosevelt, no doubt passing by on his way to his home on Campobello Island. Just off of Lubec, Maine,

Campobello belongs to New Brunswick, Canada. It may be the only case in American history where the elected president actually resided in Canada. As complicated as it sounds, the two nations managed to make it work and it remains, to this day, as one of history's best examples of multi-national cooperation.

On the wall by the fireplace hung ancient, yellowed documents, one proclaiming the building's official status as a full-fledged United States Post Office, May 21, 1891. The post office had been closed twenty years ago with the downsizing of hundreds of Maine post offices. *"Yessuh,"* spoke Bernie as he leaned toward the old frame, *"lots of old Maine post offices now serve as restaurants, offices, homes . . . all sorts of things. By the way, the oldest wokin Post office is ovah in Castine. Been theyah since 1830!"*

A rosy-cheeked women in her fifties appeared carrying menus and water. She had her hair up in a bun strategically speared with a yellow "HB" pencil. "Hello," she announced with a friendly smile. "I'm Sally . . . owner, cook, waitress, janitor . . . whatever it takes. For today's specials, we have pistachio chicken salad, fresh Lobster salad on homemade croissants, goat cheese, bacon, and broccoli quiche and we also have fresh biscuits with strawberries and cream, strawberry pie and raspberry tarts. And then there are lots of other tasty treats on the menu."

As the hungry travelers "ewed and awed" at the delicious possibilities, a tall lean man entered the front door. He had to stoop to avoid hitting his head. Removing his baseball cap revealed a tanned bald head, deep-set brown eyes, and a grey goatee surrounding a wide friendly smile. He had already patted Bernie on the shoulder and was now extending his hand to the remainder of the crew. "Noel," he offered . . . "Bernie and Jim go way back with me. They helped me create a real studio out of a hundred-year-old chicken house up in Blue Hill. You would never know it was a chicken house except when it rains!" At that point, Noel grinned and held his generous nose and they all broke into laughter.

Hal's mind was spinning. He glanced at Liz, and she was thinking the same thing. The face was unique . . . and hard to forget but it was when he began to talk . . . his resonant voice and inflections revealed his identity. They had seen him on too many PBS Christmas specials to count! Hal extended his hand: "Hal . . . this is my wife, Liz. I'm the new pastor over at Appleton Community. Sorry to say this . . . you probably get this a lot . . . but Liz and I have loved your music since we were in college. We're big fans."

Noel Paul Stookey smiled and graciously acknowledged their kind words. "Welcome to Maine. I moved here back in the late seventies . . . and I am still learning the ropes. I moved here from Manhattan . . . so I can relate. These are great people . . . but be careful, they will play tricks on you!" Hal laughed and explained briefly about the salt water in his pulpit glass.

As the meal progressed Hal could hardly believe that this was Paul of the legendary Peter, Paul, and Mary. He had managed to put the fame of the music industry on hold and had become part of the life and fabric of coastal Maine. His humor, stories and wit were a treat and as time flew by unnoticed, the short lunch became a three-hour feast. As he stood to leave, Noel bent one more time over the guests: "I'm at the Rockport Opera House next month with Denny Bouchard and Tim Sample. Stop by the ticket office, I'll make sure you guys have good seats . . . my treat!"

Stepping outside, a flock of seagulls squawked overhead and headed toward the open water. Hal was reaching out to bid their guest farewell when he noticed one of the seagulls had just bombarded Noel's collar most disrespectfully. Betsy jumped in, embarrassed. *"Oh deayuh! Look what that seagull did on yowah shirt collah! Now don't you move. I'll run inside and grab a roll of toilet papah!"* "Dow . . . " interjected Bernie *"don't you make no nevahmind about it . . . by the time you get that papah that bird will be a mile from heyah!"* Noel roared with laughter and pulled out a handkerchief to clean up the "fowl" deposit.

The late afternoon sun and gentle wind made for smooth sailing back to Lincolnville Beach. As the Baby Titanic gently rolled with the swells, Bernie poked Hal and nodded at the women. They were dead asleep leaning on each other. Hal winked as he took a picture of the sleeping beauties with his cell phone.

Chapter 25

Firestorm

Hal sat at his desk, his hand trembling, tears welling up in his eyes. The pink stationery he Held between his fingers exuded a soft scent of perfume . . . but the text smelled like the very smoke of hell. "Isn't it interesting," he mused . . . "how something so innocent and dainty can, with a few pen strokes, be transformed into something so hateful, so evil, so life-changing and so destructive?"

Hal had been warned there would be days like this. Although he often mentioned publicly that he had an "open door policy," those who would sow the most discord never came to talk face to face . . . but chose rather to drop their venom into the mailbox, hit "send" on their e-mail account, or, as in this case, slide a letter under the office door. One phrase adorned the pink flowered envelope: "For the Pastor: Confidential."

The letter was an accusation of impropriety on the part of Brad, Appleton's Worship Pastor. Word had been circulating among "certain concerned parties" that Brad had damaged the reputation of the Lord and of the church by being seen in various public settings in the company of an "indiscreet young woman, great with child and of questionable moral stature." The words made Hal boil with anger.

Grabbing a book, he had been reading, he flung it at the far wall where it landed with a smack. "Stupid, old cows! What hogwash! All of it, hogwash!" Walter, who had been sleeping by the door and startled by the ruckus, was now running in circles woofing like an old steam engine. After regaining his composure, Hal tentatively opened his office door and peered out. He breathed a sigh of relief when he saw Ruth had stepped out to lunch and he was alone in the building. It was just him, Walter, and God in this big building . . . and he was quite sure God was on his side in this fight. His mind went back to the famous "ink bottle" stain on the wall of Wartburg Castle in Germany. As he raged a personal battle against Satan and his evil doings . . . young Martin Luther had also slung an object at the wall. Visitors to the famed castle always seek out the stain . . . the evidence of young Martin's battle with Satan.

The red-hot reverend sat with his feet on the desk, arms folded behind his head trying to think. The words of Paul to the believers in Ephesus came to mind. An elderly Paul warned that the fight we fight isn't about people . . . *"We are not fighting against flesh-and-blood enemies, but against evil rulers and authorities of the unseen world, against mighty powers in this dark world, and against evil spirits in the heavenly places. (Ephesians 6:12)"*

As angry as he was with this misguided lady and those in league with her, she was, he realized, not the enemy . . . but rather the victim of the enemy. The letter was cruel, accusatory, and demanding. It had been signed: "In sincere Christian love, Evelyn Brown, member since 1968."

This woman of age, stature, and influence claimed to have a group of "concerned" members backing her, and "they" (whoever "they" were) demanded Brad's dismissal. Hal knew Brad . . . and he knew Samantha and he would have none of this. Brad was a young man who really wanted to live well and serve God with his musical and leadership gifts. Samantha was trying to live right on the heels of a string of bad choices. She had confessed her failures and was now facing life as a single "soon-to-be" mother. She had met with her estranged father, and it looked like there was progress, maybe even a possible reconciliation . . . and now this! These busybodies would have to be dealt with . . . soon and head-on.

Hal knew he needed wisdom. This could become an out-of-control "firestorm" devastating the church or causing the pastor to walk away in discouragement. Firestorms often lead to a church "split" and divide both the congregation and the community. These kinds of tragedies even cause people to abandon their faith and walk away from ever attending any church, ever again. Hal knew this was war . . . and it was very dangerous. He got on his knees, put his head and elbows on the chair seat, and began to pray. He would stay in that position for as long as it would take . . . until the Lord gave him some direction. He could not move ahead in his own wisdom. He needed God's help.

Later that afternoon, Hal stood, stretched his cramped limbs . . . opened his office door, and asked his secretary to set up an emergency meeting of the church board "ASAP." About four o'clock, Ruth knocked on Pastor Tuttle's door to announce that they were still waiting on one member as he was traveling but it looked like it could happen at the parsonage, Friday night at seven. She then added a "PS" that she would have the ladies of the "Missions Committee" bake sweets for the meeting. Hal grinned and thanked her profusely. Then as he got back to his study notes, he whispered: "Lord, thanks for good, kind people like Ruth!" He then paused and added: "Oh yeah, Lord please help Evelyn Brown and her friends to see the truth in this situation. I know, that with your help, this can all turn out for good!"

Chapter 26

Powwow at the Parsonage

Ever since accepting the call to serve Appleton Community Church, Hal had been dreading trouble. He had been fairly warned that this kind of thing happened, and it could either make the leadership better . . . or bitter. Hal and Liz had spent the last couple of days either on their knees or on the phone seeking counsel from wise pastors who had graduated from "the school of hard knocks."

As the church board sat in a circle, Hal explained that Jim Dinsmore had been briefed by his brother Bernie and had sent some counsel via e-mail. Hal began to read: "Dear Hal and my friends at Appleton, I wish I were there in person to help you through this. Be aware that Pastor Osgood is bathing this very meeting in prayer and is trusting God to turn this all around for His good. This will be a crucial test of the level of unity Pastor Osgood had built up in you as leaders and it is a test for your new pastor.

Let me challenge you as a church to move in a bold direction. For many years Appleton Community has talked about love and forgiveness . . . well now is when the rubber meets the road. You know, my brothers, some church folk wouldn't even give Jesus himself a break. They'd criticize something about him . . . like the Pharisees who always were looking for a way to take Jesus down. Remember this: you can please some of the people some of the time, but you can't please all the people all of the time. Anybody who holds an elected office . . . be it a pastor or politician, will never make everybody happy.

There are, in my opinion, five people here that you need to be concerned about: First, you must do right by what you know God would want

. . . so put Him first. Secondly, Pastor Hal, you need to be true to your calling. Be the leader God has called you to be . . . so trust God and do right. The third person is Brad. You need to be fair and compassionate to him. Stick up for him and you all will have a friend for life. A lesser pastor would throw somebody else under the bus just to save their own skin . . . which is a flat-out sin and I know that Hal is above that. The fourth person here is Samantha. She is probably carrying a load of guilt knowing that she has stirred up a hornet's nest. You need to help her get rid of that guilt. She is an innocent party in this. Help her to stay sweet. Now last but not least, Satan has worked in the mind and heart of our dear sister Evelyn. I have known her all of my life . . . and she is a good lady but easily swayed or convinced about issues. Love her, forgive her . . . but above all speak truth to her. I pray you will be able to make the truth about this situation clear to her. I pray you will win back a sister and God can greatly use her."

Hal looked around the room. His lips parched, his throat dry . . . not sure what to say . . . or if he could. Billy Munroe cleared his throat and began: *"Well suh, Dollie and me was thinkin . . . and askin the good lahwd what he'd have us do about this. Since none of us ah pehrfect . . . and we all came through grace . . . how can we do other?"* A great cacophony of *"Yessah,"* *"You got it right chummy,"* and *"Well suh!"* rose up from this normally sedate group.

What happened next took Hal and Liz by surprise. For almost an hour, the men brainstormed about a "town hall meeting" where the truth would be brought out, and this thorny matter could finally and forever be laid to rest. Hal, startled by their decisive actions to seek reconciliation and forgiveness . . . sat blubbering like a baby. He had been prepared for a difficult meeting to convince the men to move on this . . . and they were not just moving . . . they were running full steam ahead!

Before you knew it a date had been set, duties assigned and the plans had been made. They held hands and committed the upcoming meeting to God . . . then they got up and made their way to the dessert table. The ladies of the Missions Committee, intent on helping make the evening a success had loaded the table high with blueberry pie, strawberry pie, three different cakes, cookies, and an entire tray of Dolly Munroes "Buckeyes," (Chocolate coated Peanut Butter balls). With the difficult business settled, and their plates loaded down, the men sat back and relaxed.

Dick Maurice stirred his coffee and looked across the room at Bud Munroe. *"Say Bud . . . "* he began, *"Have you done any parachutin' lately?*

Pastor Harold turned his head in surprise and said: "Parachuting? You're kidding me?" Looking at Bernie he detected a sly grin and a "here it comes" look in his eyes. Hal knew he was about to get reeled in. There was nothing that Bud loved more than pulling the wool over his "Flatlander" pastor's eyes . . . but Hal could not resist. Hal grinned and said: "OK . . . you've got me! Go on"

Bud chewed contentedly on a buckeye, crossed his long legs, and began: *"Well suh . . . Dolly and I decided that life on the pond t'was a bit slow . . . so we went for a Saturday drive and would up at the Dairy Queen in Rockland. Well don't ya know there was a postah on the wall that said: "Parachute lessons, $10 at the Owl's Head airpot." So Dolly and I thought 'By golly, this might just be the ticket', so we went and met Stan Watson. He's the pilot and instructah all rolled inta one. Seemed pretty straight forward. He said when I say jump, you jump, count to ten then pull the ripcod. So anyhow we got up where we could see from Bath to Belfast as clear as can be . . . and he yelled jump . . . and so I did. Dolly would be right along behind me. Well, yes suh . . . I counted to ten and pulled on the ripcod . . . and by cracky that chute opened up just beautiful and I just floated down real gentle like. Well I waited and waited for Dolly and it seemed like fowahevah . . . but by golly she blew by me . . . musta been doin a hundad miles an howah! She was a pullin and a pullin on the ripcod . . . and nothin seemed to be happenin! Well . . . I looked down and I could see past heh . . . and there was a man . . . comin straight up of the face of the eath! And as they met I could heah Dolly yelling: 'Say . . . do ya know anything about parachutes?' To which the feller replied 'No I don't . . . do ya know anything about gas stoves?"* With that Bud doubled over in laughter, slapped his knee, and repeated: *"Do ya know anything about gas stoves?"*

This one caught Hal by surprise and, along with his guests . . . roared with laughter until tears filled his eyes. Once again, Bud had lured him in, set the hook, and reeled him completely in. This time Hal loved it. When he found the time, he would write that one down!

As the last car exited the parking, Liz squeezed Hal's hand and whispered: "Pretty good bunch of guys you've got there." Hal smiled but was unable to speak. It had been one of those rare nights when a pastor gets to be a spectator to God at work rather than trying to make something happen. Something was happening . . . but it had little if anything to do with him. The days ahead would have challenges. His "to-do" list included meeting with Brad, and Samantha and making sure that Evelyn Brown and her backers would attend the "Town hall meeting." In his heart, Hal felt a knot tighten. He knew this had the potential to be a knockdown, drag-out confrontation . . . unless God had other plans.

Chapter 27

Dealing With the Mess

The ten days between the arrival of the pink letter and the "town hall" meeting were perhaps the busiest and most stressful days he had ever experienced. The meeting with Brad at the diner had gone as well as could be expected. He assured Hal there had never been any hint of impropriety. Brad added they had become good friends, and they were spending time together as good friends. "Well, I am sure she could use a friend these days," interjected Hal. "You can say that again. She has no one in her life save for Gladys and me. Some of the church ladies get her involved in outings and stuff . . . but she is getting rounder!" Brad laughed as he said it. "Oh, by the way, Pastor Hal, she did meet with her dad. He was pretty angry . . . mostly with himself for failing Sam and his family." Hal pressed the issue. "Do you think there may be a future for you two?" Brad reddend . . . "Well, I do think a lot of her. I am not sure about the readymade family deal. That wasn't what I was expecting in life . . . no pun intended." "Look Brad don't let this craziness pressure you. Just take your time. Promise me you won't resign over this false accusation. I need you, man."

Brad sat looking down at the table for what seemed like a full minute. Looking up he spoke: "Pastor Hal, I know that God wants me to be here at Appleton . . . and I won't go unless He leads me. I want to finish up my studies so maybe . . . I will survive this. Next fall I will take a couple of classes at the Bible College in Bangor. It's a drive . . . might have to trade the monster truck for a little gas sipper? Anyhow, I know I want to be in ministry . . . as for Sam . . . well we will work on that. Like I said . . . If we survive this!" Hal reached out and clasped his hand firmly. "We will, Son. We will."

Hal and Liz had met with Sam out at the farm. Gladys was in particularly good spirits. She managed to serve fresh strawberry shortcakes with fresh whipped cream and a pot of coffee before discreetly disappearing out to the porch. They could hear the rhythmic creaking of the old rocker as off in the distance a teenage boy on Gladys' riding mower made large passes at the football field-sized lawn.

As Harold did his best to explain the letter and its contents, and not surprisingly a river of tears came as Samantha sobbed. None of this had been her fault and the criticism was undeserved. As Liz held her, she was encouraged to wait . . . be patient, it would all work out. At one point, Sam blurted out: "Well I'm surprised anybody would think Brad would even want me! Just look at me . . . I'm as big as a house!" Hal reached out, squeezed her hand, and announced quite frankly: "You my dear are a very attractive and smart young lady. Don't be surprised if some handsome young guitar player sweeps you off your feet!" Samantha, who had been crying her eyes out, exploded with laughter . . . causing her nose to bubble in a most unattractive fashion! Liz reached out and wiped her nose like a mother would for a child. Hal laughed and added, "Well, that might happen if you can keep your nose clean!" Together they laughed, briefly forgetting the misery brought by the pink flowered envelope.

That Sunday they all felt like they were walking on eggshells. Although many had not sensed anything was wrong, Hal, the church board, Brad, and Samantha took extra care not to get into any protracted conversations about church matters and all were warned to curb any conversation that might arise about any rumors or whispers about "scandal, accusations or impending resignations." Fortunately, nothing was said. Evelyn did poke her neighbor in the ribs when board chairman Dick Maurice announced the upcoming meeting. Not "spilling the beans," Dick did urge the membership to "please attend" as there were important matters to discuss. On the way out of church, Evelyn and some of her friends seemed to be particularly jovial. Hal could not help but wonder what the tone of next Sunday's meeting would be . . . or if he and Brad would even have their jobs when all of this was over.

Chapter 28

Showdown on Appleton Ridge

Hal spent most of Friday fidgeting, checking his notes, and going over all of the eloquent arguments he would make. He visualized himself as a dazzling attorney, wowing the jury with his astute defense and revealing cross-examination. At about four, he got a call from Pastor Jim in Eden Prairie, Minnesota.

The familiar voice began with: "Been thinking and praying for you friend! Look Hal don't try too hard to have your way tonight. Let God lead . . . and you might be surprised what could happen. I need to tell you this: Debbie and I have been praying that this might be the greatest opportunity for growth that Appleton Community Church might ever have. Think about it. What opportunity has the church ever had to make a clear statement about who they really want to be? They don't want to be known as judgmental, rock-throwing Pharisees. I believe many have been waiting for such a time as this to show how much they really can care for and love hurting people."

Hal sat on the rear deck, one hand scratching Walter's ear, the other holding a cold iced tea. Liz slid her hand across his shoulder and spoke softly: "Penny for your thoughts . . . " "Oh, you'll need at least a twenty for all that's spinning around my brain. You know, ever since Pastor Jim's call, I feel strangely calm. I really believe this is going to be a life-changing meeting." Hal and Liz sat watching the shadows change in the field behind their home.

Putting her finger up to her lips, Liz nodded towards a Whitetail doe serenely chewing on some grass, her short tail flicking to keep the summer flies away. Hal sat and watched quietly as the lyrics to one of his favorite worship tunes worked through his soul: *As the deer panteth for the water, So my soul longeth after thee. You alone are my heart's desire. And I long to worship thee.* Hal could almost hear the congregation joyfully launch into the chorus: *You alone are my strength, my shield. To you alone may my spirit yield. You alone are my heart's desire. And I long to worship thee.* There, on the back porch, these words came alive for Hal. It was indeed true. Tonight, God would be his strength and shield. He would need special strength and protection.

Looking at his watch he rose slowly and announced: "Battle Stations, all hands on deck!" to which Liz smartly replied: "Don't overreact Pastor Tuttle. Remember what the old missionary William Carey said: *'Expect great things from God and attempt great things for God!'*" Bowing his head in mock defeat Hal retorted: "Touché . . . my fair bride . . . touché."

By seven o'clock the church parking lot was full. As Hal and Liz walked toward the church, they were amazed at the number of members who had reacted. Hal smiled his wiggly Charlie Brown smile and said in a low voice: "Hmmm . . . must be a bake sale!"

Standing behind the pulpit, Hal noticed there was not a free seat. He turned to the board members who had seated themselves behind him at a long table with microphones smiled and whispered: "The place is full, maybe we should take an offering?" This drew laughter and cajoling from the board. Some sitting close to the front seemed irritated they were not included in the humor and could be heard querying each other: "What did he say? What are they laughing at?"

Hal was grateful for a leadership team that could smile, even laugh under duress. This would set the tone for the meeting. "Best to start out with a smile!"

Stepping up to the podium, Hal welcomed everyone and opened his bible, taking out a pink flowered envelope. Evelyn Brown and a row of blue-haired cronies could be seen visibly smiling and looking expectantly at each other. This would be their moment of triumph. Godliness, piety, and purity would reign supreme. They would show this wicked and perverse generation a thing or two about what it means to stand for truth in a day of immorality!

After a brief prayer, Hal began: "Friends, this church has stood here on Appleton Ridge since 1816. For almost two hundred years, God, by His Spirit, has led this fellowship through thick and thin. You have had many fine, Godly pastors . . . and scores of great leaders to assist him. I have only been your pastor for a short while . . . while many of our elders and deacons have served your church for decades. It is for that reason I have invited the church board to join me here on the platform. I will explain the situation, then I will turn it over to the board who will make several statements, and explain their decision and then you may, one at a time and in order step up to the mike in the center aisle, state your name and question. The board will answer your questions. I will not. They are your representatives, they are long-time members like you and I, as the pastor, will not rule on today's matter."

A rumble of conversation rose up among the pews. No doubt the accusers were hoping to take advantage of a new, inexperienced minister. It would not happen. They would have to deal with their peers . . . Mainers who were tough as old leather, cunning as foxes and they were not about to let anybody trip up the good progress of Appleton Community Church!

Hal waited for the hubbub to subside, then he took out the letter and began to read. You could have heard a pin drop. Toward the end of the letter the silence was punctuated by a rather audible "honk" as Samantha blew her nose. No doubt she was crying again. Liz had sat beside her and was fishing for something in her purse. Hal concluded it must be more Kleenexes she was looking for. After he finished reading, he folded the letter, returned it to the envelope, and returned it to his Bible.

He looked up, his tone serious and continued: "We take these accusations seriously. I have met with the parties concerned and have made them aware of this letter. I have been most impressed with the attitude of those involved. We have met and I have yet to interact with two young people more committed to doing the right thing." He looked at the board members and nodded.

Dick Maurice tapped on the microphone and after loudly clearing his throat began to speak. "*Friends . . . I want to staht off this evenin by readin a remindah from the Bible. It's found in John chaptah eight. Yowah welcome to read along . . . theyahs a pew Bible right in front of you.*" There was a considerable shuffling of paper as many took up his offer to read along. Dick began to read: "*3 As he was speaking, the teachers of religious law and the Pharisees brought a woman who had been caught in the act of adultery. They put her in front of the crowd.4 "Teacher," they said to Jesus, "this woman was caught in the act of adultery. 5 The law of Moses says to stone her. What do you say?" 6 They were trying to trap him into saying something they could use against him, but Jesus stooped down and wrote in the dust with his fin-ger. 7 They kept demanding an answer, so he stood up again and said, "All right, but let the one who has never sinned throw the first stone!" 8 Then he stooped down again and wrote in the dust. 9 When the accusers heard this, they slipped away one by one, beginning with the oldest, until only Jesus was left in the middle of the crowd with the woman. 10 Then Jesus stood up again and said to the woman, "Where are your accusers? Didn't even one of them condemn you?" 11 "No, Lord," she said. And Jesus said, "Neither do I. Go and sin no more."*

"Here," began Dick *"we have the perfect example of how Jesus handled those who sinned. Let's make that easier to understand . . . so how about we use the term 'Mess up,' or 'Blew it?' Nowayah in this stohry does Jesus tell heh 'that's OK deauh' . . . No suh . . . She knows she did wrong . . . and Jesus knows it too. What he does say is 'I don't condemn you . . . go and don't do it again.'*

At this point, Dick turned to Dave Wallace. Dave, a former teacher from Boston, would add a certain finesse to their presentation. Leaning into the microphone, Dave spoke softly but clearly: "Thank you, Dick. The John eight passage is so relevant as it speaks to the key issue here which is forgiveness." Sitting in the "bishop" chair, center stage, Hal couldn't be more pleased. These guys were doing a spectacular job! "If you will permit me, let me add the flavor of Romans chapter eight that says this about God's chil-dren: *"There is no condemnation for those who belong to Christ Jesus."* What that tells me is this: If you belong to Christ . . . there is no condemnation for you." At that point, Dave looked over to Bud Munroe.

Bud, best described as big-hearted with rough edges, stood up yanked the microphone out of its holder with a loud "pop" and began: *"Well suh . . . we waz talkin it ovah and it seemed cleyah as day that we'd best not get involved in trying to hog-tie God. I remembah from Sunday school right in this verah building . . . that John said somethin like this: 'If we confess owah sins . . . He is faithful and just and will fowahgive us owah sins . . . and make us clean . . . "* Bud looked over at Pastor Hal and asked, "Am I close reverend?" Smiling Hal replied, "Spot on Bud . . . that's it!"

Bud continued: *"Well we all know that Brad and Samanther are belie-vahs . . . and since that is true . . . we got no business trying to hog tie God. When He forgives . . . well, by golly he forgives!"* A mighty roar came up from the congregation. After a few moments Bud began again: *"Wellsuh . . . theyahs a mattah that needs to be cleahed up right heyah . . . right now. We all know Samanther made a big mistake . . . and she knows it. She knows it every minute . . . every day . . . it's right theyah in front of huh . . . and she has taken care of that with the Lawd. She didn't do anything wrong by spending time with Brad . . . frankly I am glad she has a shoulder to lean on. I think we have failed huh miserably . . . I would like to ask that we . . . as a chuch . . . commit to beyin a real, loving, supportive family to Sam and her little baby. That little one is due in Septembah . . . and instead of us gatherin to throw rocks . . . let's be her family! All of those in favah . . . please stand."*

Hal watched in astonishment as the entire church . . . Evelyn and her blue-haired cronies stood together. Hal could not contain himself. He raised his arms and whispered: *"Thank you Lord!"* All over the sanctuary people began to weep. Some clapped their hands, and some laughed. Hal looked down to see several women embracing Samantha who was, of course, sobbing uncontrollably.

After a full five minutes, Bud tapped on the microphone and spoke: *"Ok . . . Ok . . . we got more stuff to deal with."* The crowd quieted. *"When Pastah Hal brought us this lettah . . . we felt it was owah duty to see if these accusations were true. So, we got a list of all of the places they had been seen togethah...and set out to make inquiries. Heyahs what we found: Every person we talked to said they had behaved perfectly. Only one person commented that she might have seen them holding hands . . . but then added that it seemed they waz prayin togethah about somethin.*

Based upon what we know to be the truth, we want to publicly cleah Brad from all of these false accusations." In response came a thunderous applause. With that, Bud put down his mike with a loud "thump," walked down to the front row where Brad had been quietly observing and gave him a mighty bear hug. Many left their seat to go and show their appreciation and support. Now Brad was balling!

Hal returned to the pulpit and tried, at first without success, to quiet the crowd. He began to speak: "Now let me address the issue of the letter. You need not know who wrote the letter. I guess by now, that person knows the truth regarding this situation. I believe they meant well by writing the letter. In time they may make their reasons public, but maybe not. Just know this dear friend, you are part of this family. From what I have seen today, you can be proud to be part of a fellowship like this that takes sin seriously . . . but forgiveness and grace even more so! Please do not separate yourself from us . . . we are a family, and we need each other." As Hal scanned the pews, he tried not to focus on Evelyn, but he did notice that her eyes were visibly moist.

Hal continued: "I am grateful for the board and their exemplary spirit today . . . " Hal's words were cut short as the congregation had turned their attention from him to Brad and Samantha, Kleenex in hand . . . walking together down the center aisle, up the steps and coming to rest beside their pastor. Hal instinctively gave them both a warm hug. Brad nodded toward the pulpit mike and Hal, smiling and unsure of where this was headed said "Sure."

"Last night Samantha and I had supper together at "The Olive Garden" in Bangor. We talked a lot about this meeting . . . and we decided we wanted to do the right thing . . . so here it is." Brad led Samantha to the left of the pulpit where all could see. He took her hand and got down on one knee. The crowd gasped. No one had been expecting this. In a shaky voice, Brad began: "Samantha . . . will you do me the honor of being my wife?" Barely audible through the wad of Kleenex held to her nose came a hoarse "I will!" Gladys Berry was on her feet, waving her cane back and forth, yelling "Thank you, Jesus!"

Now Hal was bawling, Liz was bawling, and the board had joined in . . . suffice it to say there was not a dry eye in the building. No one could have seen this coming! After a protracted time of revelry, Hal tapped on the mike and announced that everybody was invited to the dining room where the party could continue their celebrations over coffee, tea homemade pie, and ice cream.

That night the church lights stayed on well after midnight . . . but more importantly, the "light of the glorious Gospel of Christ" shone brightly with forgiveness, grace, and reconciliation in Appleton, Maine.

Chapter 29

A Jewel of a Lady

The Baby Titanic gently rolled and bobbed as Hal and Brad flicked the tips of their fishing rods, hoping for a bite. They had been fortunate and tonight there would be fresh Mackerel on the grill along with "Peaches and Cream" boiled corn, potato salad, and a spinach, nut, and cheese salad. For a moment Harold was lost in the thought of hot, buttered corn that would run down his chin and make a mess . . . but he didn't care. Summer in Maine was short, sunny, and begged to be enjoyed.

Brad gently hummed a new worship chorus he was working on for the next Sunday. Yes, there would be a next Sunday . . . and thanks to God's grace and the sweetness of the kind people of Appleton Community Church, there would likely be many more Sundays. The terrible conflict caused by the pink envelope had momentarily put everyone's dreams and plans on hold. Even Pastor Harold had questioned his future, but truth and grace had prevailed. Looking over at Samantha gently leaning back, relaxed, smiling in conversation with Liz, Brad was momentarily overcome, his eyes stinging. He squeezed them tight to fight back the tears and looked away in embarrassment. If Hal or anyone noticed, nothing was said. This was a day to soak in the sun, relax, and put the events of the past two weeks behind them.

Suddenly there was a great and exciting chatter from Samantha and Liz in the stern. They were aflutter about something and were leaning precariously over the transom. Hal and Brad had barely placed their rods in their holders when they heard a loud "arhhh arhhh arhhh" that sounded like either a Beagle baying or a carpenter working with a rusty saw. No more than a yard from the boat a large, grey seal had stuck his head up and was begging loudly for a fishy snack. These friendly creatures have even been known to climb aboard pleasure boats to seek food and have their bellies scratched! "Hal, toss him one of your Mackerels...You've got tons!" pleaded Liz who could no more resist this gregarious marine critter than turn Walter down for a chewy treat. "OK . . . softie," replied Hal tossing an iridescent fish towards the seal, who with the ease of a circus performer, caught the fish mid-air and disappeared instantly below the surface.

"That was cool!" squealed Samantha. "When I was a kid there was a seal that lived on a specially built raft in Rockport harbor. He . . . I think he was called André and had been orphaned so a local family raised him. They even made a movie about him in the nineties . . . it was called "André" . . . I think. Anyhow there are lots of seals around here. The big sharks love them! Harold who was now crouched near Liz did his best Jaws theme "Da dun . . . da dun . . . da dun" and grabbed Liz by the ankle to which she screeched . . . causing them all to go into fits of laughter.

Back at the house, the men relaxed and enjoyed the late afternoon sun as the women cleared away the dishes and put on a pot of tea. The grilled fish, the hot, buttered corn . . . everything had been superlative. Hal, crossing his legs leaned confidingly toward Brad and spoke in low tones: "Brad . . . thanks for hanging with us today. Don't hurry off, I know Samantha is a bit tired . . . but Liz has one small surprise."

Liz, with Sam in tow, appeared with two wooden trays heavily laden with tea and small white plates heaped high with hot out-of-the-oven biscuits, and mashed strawberries smothered in whipped cream. Brad grinned at Hal, raised his eyebrows, and uttered "Dude!" "Right back atcha!" whispered Hal. It was true he had indeed married the best woman in the world. But . . . since guys don't verbalize their emotions well . . . "Dude" would be as close as Brad could get to a public endorsement of Liz's awesomeness.

The late afternoon sun was sinking low over their backs to the west, casting shadows from the church steeple across the parsonage lawn and the deck where they were reclining. Almost imperceptibly a white Audi pulled into the parking lot between the house and the church. Brad leaned forward but could not see who it was. Looking to Hal, Brad spoke: "Hey Pastor Hal and Liz . . . you have visitors. I need to drop Sam off at the farm. Without speaking a word Hal looked at Brad and held up his index finger, indicating he should wait. In reply, Brad nodded and sat back, once again focusing his attention on the strawberry shortcake.

Evelyn Brown rounded the corner of the parsonage and placed her foot on the first step as Liz warmly met her, took her hand, and led her to an empty chair next to Harold. He stood and gave her a warm hug, which she reciprocated with gladness. Brad and Samantha were stunned . . . nevertheless, they both stood and extended their hands. Evelyn shaking their hands showed emotion and seemed a bit shaky. Jumping in Hal began: "Monday morning Evelyn came by my office, and we had a great conversation. She asked if I would help her find a way to apologize to you both and I invited her to join us here on the deck. I will stop talking and let her say what's on her mind."

In a quivering voice, the elderly woman began: "What I did . . . the way I did what I did . . . the accusations were all wrong. Oh . . . I feel like such a miserable old troublemaker . . . and I am so sorry. I had imagined things that weren't true. Some of my senior friends put together bits and pieces they had picked up in the village . . . and well . . . it was wrong." Tears were now running down her cheeks, and she struggled to speak. True to form, Samantha was now bawling . . . and Liz had joined her. "Would you...could you . . . both of you . . . could you find it in your hearts to ever forgive this foolish old busybody?"

Brad and Samantha rushed forward almost knocking the frail woman over. They had wrapped their arms around her and were weeping with joy. As they sobbed, Walter instinctively sensed something was happening . . . and began to lick Evelyn's hand. This caused her to laugh and return his affection with a chuckle and a "Yes . . . even Walter forgives me!" They all laughed and hugged as they wiped away their tears.

Gaining her composure, Evelyn sat down, patted her wet eyes, and looked intently at them. "I was asking the Lord about a practical way I might help you . . . and here is what He showed me." Reaching into her purse Evelyn brought out an antique red velvet box. "Brad, I think I may have pushed you into making a decision you probably weren't ready for. I know it is hard for young people like you two to afford certain things. I am an old woman . . . and I have no one to leave things to. When I was twenty-five my late husband Edward gave me this diamond ring." As she opened the box she whispered: "It was his grandmother's and came from Russia. I had it appraised many years ago and back then it was worth ten thousand dollars." As she held the open box the entire group gasped in amazement at the large, brilliant, white oval diamond. To say it was stunning would have been an understatement.

Evelyn had pulled a chair over in front of Samantha and gently slid the enormous diamond onto her finger. Samantha was now sobbing so hard she could hardly breathe. Brad had placed an arm around her and was rocking her gently back and forth. "Well, frankly," announced Evelyn, "I think it looks a whole lot better on her pretty young finger than hiding in the darkness of my sock drawer!" Samantha leaned forward and responded with a prolonged, wordless hug. Sometimes there are just no words . . . and this was one of those times.

Chapter 30

A "Day at the Fayuh."

Since its inception in 1869, the Union Fair is "The" Maine event for the whole family. With its agricultural exhibits, stock car races, baking contests, concerts, and various rides and activities, no one gets left out. A large part of the fair's success can be attributed to the annual blueberry festival. The virtual "holy grail" of blueberry cuisine hosts a cooking contest for all things blueberry. One of the spectacles that always draws both laughter, and a large crowd is the blueberry pie eating contest. It was this very event that would prove to be the good Reverend Tuttle's undoing.

The three couples: Hal and Liz, Bud and Dolly, and Bernie and Debbie strolled through the exhibits and food vendors. Hal was jubilant in his discovery of a life-long friend: fried dough. Every year growing up, Hal could hardly wait for the Minnesota State Fair in St. Paul. It seemed that every year the concession stands produced stranger and stranger fare: deep-fried cheese curds, chocolate-dipped frozen bananas, and deep-fried Snickers bars. Strangely, he could always count on fried dough . . . and here it was . . . in Union, Maine! As he chewed on it, Liz turned away in embarrassment . . . only to turn back and pass Hal a tissue. He had unknowingly covered the end of his nose with the white powdered sugar, making him look a bit like a circus clown.

Bud jabbed his friend and pastor in the ribs and exclaimed: *"Well . . . yessuh . . . theyuhs just what we need! The all-you-can-eat wild blueberry pie contest . . . Ayuh, somebody could win a new shotgun and by golly, it could be me. I ate six pies last yeah! My beeyad was blue for a week."* Bernie jumped in: *"Come on chummy . . . let's do it!"*

They had Hal in tow as the women squealed with delight. This would be fun . . . and certainly worth a laugh or two. The first prize was a new shotgun, so the stakes were high. The entrance fee of five dollars went to the Knox County Food Bank . . . so no matter the outcome, it would all be for a good cause. The rules were simple, your hands would be tied behind your back, and you could only eat sitting down, no tools . . . just your mouth . . . and it would get messy!

The three sat side by side with other contestants. The assistants placed the pies in front of the contestants and the judge blew the start whistle. They would have five minutes and the winner would be the one who would eat the most pies . . . and keep them down. I won't go into details about some rather spectacular disqualifications in the past!

The whistle blew, the crowd cheered, and they were off. It was obvious from the start that Bernie and Bud had done this before. They scooped the blueberries skillfully with their tongues, slurping in a mound of the blue concoction. Hal, with no previous experience, was attempting to find something that worked. He was making a mess of it and had blueberry pie filling in his nose, eyebrows, and hair and somehow, had managed to get some under his left eye. The locals were beating the tar out of him and when Bernie looked over at Hal, he began to laugh and snorted some of the mixture up his nose . . . which he quickly blew back out and was forced to deal with the consequences. The crowd roared with approval. The grosser it got, the louder they cheered. Bud was doing a bang-up job, but it looked like Bernie had a slight edge on him.

As the whistle blew a great cry came up from the crowd. Their hands were untied, and each contestant was handed a clean towel. Hal needed three or four towels as he was a mess! They cleaned blueberries and a purple-blue gunk from every possible orifice above the neck . . . the judge tapped on the mike and then announced the winner. "Ahem . . . *testing one two . . . testing one two . . . can you all heah me? Is this thing on?*" To which hoots and hollers came back from the crowd. He paused briefly to adjust his reading glasses. "*Havin eatin seven wicked big pies . . . the winnah of this yeah's wild blueberry pie contest is Bernie Dinsmohaw from ovah in Appleton!*" Bernie grinned, stood, and nodded as the crowd applauded loudly. "*Bernie can pick up his new Remington 870 shotgun ovah at the Coastal Hadwayuh stowah in Camden.*" Again, the crowd applauded, and Bernie waved in acknowledgement.

Walking through the crowd the three drew suspicious looks for their abundant purple stains. Bernie was on cloud nine and could have cared less if he was purple from head to toe . . . he had won the shotgun of his dreams! Bud was, as he put it: *"Fullah than a bedtick"* and produced gurgles and equally interesting noises with every step. *"Well Dolly that about done me in . . . I think we should call it a day . . . and I feel like pumped up bagpipe."* To which Dolly laughed and shot back: *"Yessuh . . . and you sound a tad bit like one too!"* The party roared with laughter.

Above the noise of the crowd a voice could be heard calling: "Oh Liz . . . Liz . . . I thought it was you!" Turning, Liz saw Nancy Stewart coming towards her. As always, Nancy was dressed to the nines with every hair in place, and makeup just right. Liz reached out, shook her hand warmly, and began to chat. Thirty seconds into the conversation, Hal strode up. Nancy stopped in mid-sentence and looked him up and down. "Good Lord man . . . what in the blazes happened to you?" Harold, just tuning into the fact that Liz had run into his secret nemesis was, once again, at a loss for words. "Umm, well, blueberries . . . blueberries." It was all he could say. Blueberries. Not "Well hello there Nancy. How are you?" Nope. He babbled like some witless soul . . . just "Blueberries." Nancy, looking down commented: "Well reverend Tuttle . . . at least your shoes match . . . even if they are slightly blue . . . or is that purple?

Walking away, Harold muttered to himself in a mocking tone: "Well reverend Tuttle, at least your shoes match." Liz laughed and leaned against him. "Boobishness . . . you can't seem to escape it!" She giggled.

Walking toward the parking area Liz froze and nudged Hal's elbow. "Hey, isn't that Samantha's dad?" The couple was coming directly toward them. There could be no avoiding them. Hal turned to Liz and spoke softly: "I don't know the woman. I hope Samantha doesn't find out he has a local girlfriend here . . . that would crush her."

"Pastor Tuttle . . . so nice to see you here. I am just up for the weekend and thought it would be nice to bring Brenda here . . . oh I am sorry, I guess you have never met. This is Samantha's mother . . . my former wife, Brenda." Harold smiled and extended his hand. "Nice to meet you," he replied. "This is my wife, Liz." As the women shook hands, Brenda smiled and said "Mrs. Tuttle, Sam has told me so much about you. We will be forever indebted to you for your kindness to our daughter . . . and to our grandson . . . or granddaughter?" Liz took a step forward and hugged Brenda. The silence was punctuated with a brief sob as Brenda spoke softly: "I know I've totally blown it as a mom . . . Sam has every reason to hate me." "Oh, she doesn't hate you!" spoke Liz. "She loves you very much. Just give her a chance."

The couple made their way toward the fairgrounds. Glancing back, Liz noticed Brenda was still weeping and had stopped behind a large exhibit tent to regain her composure. As they climbed into the SUV, Hal and Liz looked incredulously at each other. Hal spoke first: "Wow . . . that was interesting! I wonder if Samantha knows that his parents are spending time together?"

Right then and there Hal and Liz stopped to intercede for John and Brenda. They focused on Brenda's need to discover faith in Christ. Reconciliation with her maker would place her on the road to reconciliation with her husband, and her children and open the door for a new and exciting world of love, forgiveness, and a renewed family life. With her priorities redirected by God, she would discover a very different family. John had been changed by faith. Samantha had been dramatically changed. She could build a relationship with her future son-in-law Brad . . . and best of all, her first grandchild. There in the grassy field behind the fairgrounds, their Toyota SUV was transformed into a holy place as Hal and Liz prayed that God would intervene in Brenda's life . . . if only.

Chapter 31

A Miraculous Yielding

The late August warmth had been replaced with cooler weather. Early mornings now brought a layer of condensation to car windshields. Soon there would be early morning frost and the required scraping. September was a month of transition. The local roads, void of tourists, were now busy with yellow school buses. Children in bright windbreakers could be seen playing under overcast skies. Change was in the air. It was no longer summer, yet not quite fall.

Gardeners were busy protecting their plants from the cold that would come. RVs, travel trailers, cabins, and boats would be readied for the long, cold winter. Water would be drained from pipes and replaced with pink coolant. Plywood covers would be screwed down to keep out the snow, wind, and above all, squirrels. A nest of these destructive critters can wreak havoc on a cabin or RV. They love to shred whatever they can dig into and make a cozy bed for the long winter. Unfortunately, they can turn a bed, mattress, or sofa into a pile of useless mulch if left to their destructive ways.

And then there was the famous Maine blue tarp. Downeasters will tell you that there are more blue tarps per capita in their state than any other in the union. When your roof leaks, don't spend a gazillion dollars to fix it. Just throw a blue tarp over it and you can save your greenbacks for another year. If you run out of garage space and no longer have room for Uncle Bob's rototiller, just park it wherever is convenient and throw a blue tarp over it. If the transmission goes on the 86' F-150 . . . no sweat, just throw a blue tarp over the old girl and you can get around to fixing her next spring . . . or whenever. The famous blue tarp has become a part of Maine folk legend. Last year a professor from the University of Maine, Orono won rave reviews for his stage play "One Blue Tarp." Maine humorist Tim Sample does a whole stand-up shtick on how a person with murderous intent could simply cover his victim in plain sight . . . say on his lawn under a blue "tahp" . . . and his misdeed would never be exposed. Apparently, no one ever looks under a blue tarp in Maine! So, as fall creeps up on the Pine state, out come the blue tarps . . . a cheap and effective way to winterize a parked car, RV, boat, etcetera.

The men of the church had been over to the parsonage all day Saturday, sealing this and that . . . spreading great gobs of caulking around drainpipes, vents, doors, and windows. Two of the deacons inadvertently drove Liz out of her mind and out of the house when they began applying layers of clear plastic to the inside windows and heating them with a hair dryer until they snapped, taught to the touch. Liz took this opportunity to leave Harold in his church office with Walter and head off to town to stock up on some last-minute items.

Pulling into the Shop n' Save, Liz grabbed a cart and whizzed down the first aisle. As she rounded the next aisle, she almost ran straight into a very pregnant Samantha pushing a cart alongside Gladys Berry. Samantha looked very uncomfortable but assured Liz all was well. She was tired of sitting and needed to get out. Gladys hovered over her like a grandmother . . . for which everyone was thankful. While Gladys puttered with the bottles of spices, Sam leaned confidingly toward Liz. "Daddy came out to the farm last night," she began. "I almost fainted. He had mom with him. I started to cry . . . well you know how I cry. And then mom cried, and dad cried . . . Gladys had to keep us all from coming unglued. But it was good. I am praying so hard. Mom said she would go to church with me if I would sit with her!" Carefully embracing the round girl, Liz whispered: "Keep praying . . . we all are!"

True to her word, the next Sunday morning Brenda Gifford sat beside her daughter Samantha in the back rear pew. Liz never bothered to ask why Sam always sat there, figuring it was simply the closest seat to the lady's room and she should make multiple forays unnoticed by the congregation.

Brad came back to introduce himself and was warmly received by an emotional Brenda. Walking away, he caught Sam's eye and winked reassuringly at her. Liz came back and sat beside them. This instantly put all three at ease and allowed them to talk about the fair. When Liz told them about

Harold and the blueberry pie-eating contest she could barely keep from going into fits of laughter and well, after all, this was church!

The worship team began with a couple of rousing "high energy" praise choruses much to Brenda's surprise. Leaning over to Samantha she whispered that she thought all they did in church was sing stuffy old hymns accompanied by an organ. Her preconceived ideas about the church seemed to be falling apart. "Wow," she thought, "this is different!" After the worship time, announcements, and offering, the pastor encouraged the children to head out to the educational wing for what he called "Junior church."

Harold welcomed everybody and, without naming to whom he was speaking, commented that visitors are always welcome and to please feel at home among your friends at Appleton Community Church. As he opened his Bible and notes he took the glass of water from the side of the pulpit. As he got it up to his mouth, he paused looking intently at something in the glass. Ever since the seawater escapade when he spoke on being the salt of the earth, Hal had double-checked the glass . . . no longer completely trusting the "Breakfast Gang." There was a quiet pause as the congregation wondered what was going on. On the top of the water was a fly, feet up buzzing in circles like a motorboat.

Looking to his right at Bernie Dinsmore, Pastor Tuttle asked: "Bernie, what is this fly doing in my water?" On cue, like a perfectly timed comedy routine, Bernie stepped up to the pulpit, looked into the glass, and proclaimed: *"Looks like the backstroke, Pastah."*

The church went wild. Bud Munroe bellowed like a harpooned hippo, slapped his knee, and yelled out: *"Yessah . . . the backstroke . . . Well, I'll be a monkey's uncle!"* The crowd roared with laughter for a full five minutes. That phrase: "Looks like the backstroke pastor" would bring a chuckle for years to come. In the meantime, Hal had to get this service back on track.

Dick Maurice had reappeared and was now bringing a clean, bug-free glass of water up to the podium. Taking a long drink, Harold smiled at Bernie, paused for effect, and launched out into his introduction. The humor had broken the ice, and his congregation was with him.

Today's sermon, he announced, was entitled "Two men, two decisions and two results." He began to unfold the story in Luke chapter twenty-three where Jesus was crucified on the cross between two condemned criminals. One man, knowing his guilt had hard words for the other criminal for mocking Jesus in unbelief. Because of the thief's belief and repentance, Jesus tells him: "Today you will be with me in heaven." "This story," continued

Harold, "is amazing because this man was guilty . . . he had blown it, failed miserably in life yet Jesus showed him forgiveness and mercy! He had never been to church, never sang a hymn, never said a prayer, never read the Bible . . . and yet, he simply believes . . . and, to use a metaphor, "runs to Jesus." The results are staggering . . . Jesus promises him eternal life!"

In the back pew, a deeply troubled Brenda mulled over the pastor's words. "Is it possible to be a Christian by just believing? Don't you have to do stuff . . . burn candles . . . give money . . . say prayers? How can this be so simple?"

At the end of the service, Harold invited anyone who would simply "Run to Jesus" to join him at the front of the auditorium. There would be no browbeating . . . no five verses of a heart-tugging hymn . . . just an offer to consider a simple kneeling and yielding to Jesus. "Yielding," Hal explained, "is how this thief discovered God's grace . . . and it is all anyone needs to do."

As the final hymn ended, Pastor Hal led the congregation in a closing prayer and benediction. Opening his eyes, he could hardly believe what he was seeing. At the far left of the stage, three women were huddled on their knees . . . Liz, Samantha, and Brenda. They had their arms around Brenda and were all weeping. As the congregation quietly exited the worship center, Hal and Brad went and joined them. Like the thief on the cross, Brenda had simply and wonderfully yielded.

Chapter 32

Grace . . . Getting What We Don't Deserve

Standing on a ladder, Liz reached high into the tree, snapping the bright red Cortland apples off the branches and passing them down to Hal, the "ladder holder." Keeping one hand in place, he slid the prized fruit into a canvas sack he had hung over his shoulder. As they moved from tree to tree in the orchard, the team had a system. Hal emptied the apples into a large wicker basket while Liz sought out a new tree. Walter's part was to christen the tree formally announcing their arrival.

According to Liz, master chef and apple picker, she would require two types of apples for her projects: Macintosh for applesauce and pies . . . and for eating, Cortland. It was impossible to resist sampling the harvest and when Hal bit into a large Cortland, it made a loud "crack" and cold juice ran down his chin. There was no disputing the fact that eating a crisp cold Maine apple directly off the tree was a feast for the senses. A store-bought apple could never replicate the aroma, texture, sweetness, and juiciness one experiences in the cool fall outdoors.

Lifting the two hampers onto their cart, the two made their way to the little cabin at the entrance to the orchard. Charlie Perkins weighed them on an old cast iron scale that had undoubtedly weighed many tons of apples here on Appleton Ridge. Hal grabbed two one-gallon jugs of Charlie's "Fresh squeezed apple cider." Charlie, a local character par excellence laughed and gave stern warning: *"Now I'll give ya fayuh wannin preacha, that theyah cidah'l put hair on yoah chest!"* "Thanks, replied Hal . . . but I don't need any more . . . but I'll be careful not to overdo it!" Liz simply grinned and raised her eyebrows recalling how a glass of this cider left her mouth feeling like she had just stood under a virtual waterfall of fresh Maine apple flavor. It was something one had to experience on a cool fall day on Appleton Ridge. Pulling a twenty from his wallet, Hal concluded his business with the orchard owner and began to lift the apples into the back of the SUV.

Back at the parsonage, Hal placed the apples on the floor while Walter headed for his water bowl. Liz listened intently to the phone's message manager. "Not enough room in the fridge for the cider . . . " spoke Harold. Raising a "shh" hand signal to Hal, Liz scribbled something intently on a yellow sticky note. Putting down the phone Liz looked serious as she spoke. "Just put the cider on the deck . . . we've got to go. Our little Samantha is in labor."

Grabbing his clergy badge for Penobscot Bay Medical Center and, with Liz in tow, headed for the car. Pressing the accelerator a bit harder than usual, the big Toyota bounced along the winding road taking them to US Route One. Liz remained silent, knowing Harold, a competent driver, very rarely pushed the limit. Pulling into the "Clergy Only" spot, Hal and Liz jumped out and headed through the wide glass doors. At the reception desk, the red-haired girl saw his ID badge and offered: "Who do you need to see reverend?" "Sam . . . Samantha Gifford . . . " Hal spoke breathlessly. Looking at her computer screen, she tapped a few keys and announced: "Third floor, maternity . . . but you will have to ask at the nurses station."

Getting off at the elevator Hal and Liz were greeted by a disheveled Brad dressed in sweats. Extending his hand, Brad stammered: "Sorry . . . I was at the gym in town when Sam called me. I drove out to the farm and picked her up. Gladys had Sam's overnight bag in hand and handed me a bag lunch . . . she is so awesome! Anyhow, Sam's in labor . . . and since we're not married, the nurses felt it was best I wait out here." Liz was back from speaking to the nurses and was holding a scrub suit and face mask. "They said I could go in. Has anybody called Brenda?" "Yeah . . . I called her a few minutes ago. She will come as soon as she can get somebody at work to replace her."

Hal and Brad hunkered down and thumbed through the copious pile of outdated magazines. Finally at the bottom of a large stack of cooking and women's magazines Hal pulled out a "Car and Driver" and announced: "Score." Brad gave him a "thumbs up" and replied "Dude!"

At about mid-afternoon, Brenda stepped off the elevator. She greeted Hal with a warm handshake but what happened next was an omen of what was to come . . . she wrapped her arms around Brad and kissed him on the cheek. "Wow!" thought Hal. "Not long ago she would have nothing to do with her daughter . . . and now she is kissing her future son-in-law! That's a God thing for sure." Brenda headed for the nurse's station and disappeared through the "Staff Only" door. Hal smiled at Brad as they sat down and relaxed like two old hound dogs on a sunny porch. Harold broke the silence: "Can you believe the change in that woman?" Brad grinned, ran his hands through his hair, and simply replied: "God . . . it's got to be. Nobody can change another person . . . Not like that."

At about six o'clock, the elevator door opened with a "ding" and John Gifford stepped into the reception area. "Hey, pastor, Brad . . . how's my Sam doin'?" "So far so good," replied Brad. "Have a seat, I'll go downstairs and grab us some coffee." Instinctively Hal pulled out his wallet and insisted that the coffee be his treat. They were just stirring the sugar and milk with the little plastic sticks when the familiar face of Doc Sullivan walked into the waiting area. He looked tired and was covered in sweat. He dropped like a stone on the brown sofa, wiped his eyes and crossed his legs. "Well Mr. Gifford," began the weary doctor, "congratulations are in order! You now have a beautiful little granddaughter. Sam is doing great, she's tired and hungry . . . and the little one is fast asleep in her mom's arms. I think my job is about done here. If anything changes the nurses will call me . . . but from what I can see this little girl is healthy and should do just fine!"

Doc Sullivan stood and as he did so, John rose up and gave the doctor a warm embrace. He suddenly stepped back blurting out "Sorry, I just had to hug you!" Doc Sullivan smiled and reassured him that many a happy parent and grandparent had done the same . . . and that was perfectly fine with him.

Later that night Samantha sat upright in her bed caressing a little pink bundle held tightly to her chest. She could barely believe that not long ago she was suicidal . . . calling this child a "mistake." She had received grace. Brad had loved her despite her imperfections . . . so had Hal and Liz, and Gladys and all of her new friends at church. Her mom and dad were also experiencing grace . . . but most of all she had received grace upon grace from God.

As she sat there, she leaned over and whispered something to Brad. He smiled and nodded. She looked around the room and tried to speak. Nothing but little squeaky noises would come out. John, Brenda, Hal, and Liz sat waiting. Brad passed her a Kleenex. She blew her nose with a "honk" and tried to speak again. This time something came out: "Because I have received grace . . . more grace than I could ever deserve . . . I want to name this little girl Hannah. I read that Hannah is the Hebrew word for grace . . . and it will always serve as a reminder that God is a good, kind God full of mercy and grace. He is not mad at us for the wrong things we do . . . he loves us despite our failures. We don't get what we deserve with God. That is grace!"

Hal walked over to the bedside and laid a hand on the small precious infant. For a few brief moments, Pen Bay Medical Center's room number 312 was transformed into a holy place where a young mother, stepfather-to-be, grandfather and grandmother, pastor, and wife proclaimed God's hand of mercy on precious little Hannah. As he prayed, Samantha wept and blew her nose. As the prayer ended, a well-meaning young nurse barged into the room carrying a tray. When she saw that the entire room was in tears, she looked around and asked is everything OK? Is the baby OK? To which Liz reached up, placed her hand on the nurse's arm, and quietly said: "Dear . . . everything is more than OK. But thanks for caring. We are all doing great!"

Chapter 33

Back on the Breakfast Bus

Harold was beginning to look forward to his sorties with the Appleton Breakfast gang. Although the fall leaves had turned bright orange, yellow, and red and there had been a morning frost, the kitchen in Gus' bus heated the mobile restaurant to a comfortable, if not cozy, temperature.

The regular crew had come out this Saturday morning though some were in full hunting garb, taking a quick breakfast break before returning to the woods. The hunting stories abounded. Dick Maurice made a comment that the hunters were so thick this year that a farmer up in Aroostook County had the deer shot right off of his tractor. "Ha, ha!" retorted Hal. "Deer . . . Deere . . . get it."

Bud Munroe looked serious. *"Ya know Pastah . . . 'Jackin's' a serious problem heyuh in Maine."* Harold looked puzzled. "What's 'Jackin?'" he inquired. *"Well suh . . . Jackin is illegal huntin. It's a big deal heyuh right up through the 'noth country." Fellers go out at night, shine a spotlight at the deeyuh . . . or moose . . . they stand still lookin at the light and then bang. That's all."* At that point, Bud's eyes took on a twinkle that Bernie, Maynard and Dick recognized. Bernie leaned over to Hal and whispered: *"Look out pastah . . . heyah comes a zingah!"*

"Well suh," Bud continued. *"A game wahden up in Greenville saw a cah comin outta the woods late at night with a big buck tied across its hood. The wahden pulls them ovah and says 'Mighty late to be in the woods ain't it boys? One feller says "Well we was in the woods . . . and we sorta got lost." At this point the wahdens got out his flashlight and he's lookin mighty close at the big buck. "Mind tellin me why on God's green earth you shot this deeyuh three* times?" One of the hunters speaks up and says: "No suh . . . we didn't shoot him three times, I promise."

At that the wahden takes his flashlight and shines it real close like at the deer. He points out that theyuh's a bullet hole in one front hoof . . . and a bullet hole in t'otha hoof . . . and a bullet hole smack dab in the middle of the crittahs forehead. Not being able to outsmaht the wahden any longah the youngah of the two puts both hands to his forehead and bellows: 'Well suh, when we tuhned on the spotlight it went like dis!'" The breakfast crew roared with laughter. All the way home Hal could see Bud Munroe, standing hunched over in Gus' bus covering his eyes with his two hands, wheezing with laughter!

Chapter 34

A Christmas to Remember

The living nativity scene had been Hal's brainchild. He had shared his vision with the deacon board and had received a very positive response. "My idea," began Hal "is to have a community event that will draw people from far and wide. Imagine that we use the big old barn and adjacent buildings on the Berry farm. I have already spoken to Gladys and she is tickled pink. We will have all manner of farm animals lent to us by Appleton's farming community. We can build a manger scene with Mary, Joseph, and Baby Jesus . . . Samantha, Brad, and baby Hannah . . . provided we put some space heaters in there.

In the evening, we can start in the big garage where we can have chairs set up, serve hot coffee, tea, and cocoa, and we can tell the Christmas story, sing carols, then lead a group through the living nativity scene. Bud says he's got a big old star that will light up . . . we can hang that high from the hayloft lift beam on the outside." All of these ideas grew grunts of approval and nods from the men. Dick Maurice looked around and proclaimed: *"You are indeed a dreamah pastah Hal . . . and we love you for it!"*

Billboards in town, newspaper ads, and even some local radio publicity helped generate excitement for this local "first." Steve Ellis, writer, and photographer came by to interview Pastor Harold and discover what the buzz was all about. After publishing a very positive piece in the Camden Herald entitled "Get ready to see something amazing!" inquiries to Ruth at the church office rose into the hundreds. The men and women of the church pulled together, the men cleaning out the barn and garage and constructing various sets while the women sewed costumes and organized food tables. It seemed like everyone at Appleton Community Church was involved.

The week before Christmas, there would be three showings a night for three nights. This was becoming a huge event . . . and Hal was sure it would give the community a connection with the local church like it had never experienced.

At 6 pm on Christmas week, it was already dark. Looking down the long driveway from the main road there appeared to be a long line of head-lights as far as the eye could see. Out on Appleton Road, Ben Libby, a Knox County Sheriff's Deputy was helping keep traffic moving. The blue and red flashing lights of his squad twinkled in the crisp winter night. Greeters with orange cone flashlights borrowed from the Fire Station directed cars to parking spots on the expansive front lawn. It was crisp and cold with a light dusting of snow underfoot.

Soon the first group was seated in the old garage, which had been magically transformed into a Christmas wonderland with large evergreens decorated and lit to perfection. Holding steaming mugs of hot cocoa and fresh cookies the group joined Hal as they sang along with the "orchestra." They tried to keep the music as simple as possible, which worked out to their benefit by providing what could best be described as a "Christmas Folk Ensemble." There were two teenage girls on violin, Marion Potter on flute, and two men playing guitars. Bud Munroe had dug out his mandolin and Ed Carlson was plucking his banjo. All in all, it created a soothing ambiance and gave Hal a good opportunity to lead into the Christmas story and then escort them in a mannerly fashion to the "manger."

In the barn, there were lots of animals: sheep, goats, chickens, a pony, one sad-eyed donkey named Eyore, and Randy Dickinson's prize Jersey, Emma. There was, without exaggeration, a most barn-like odor. In the cor-ner was the full-size manger scene. Although there was no doubt the baby Jesus had not been bathed in the glow of Halogen industrial lights . . . it was somehow surreal. When baby Hannah decided she was hungry and began to scream . . . it only added to the realism. After all, would not the Christ child have cried . . . or filled his diapers? Was Jesus not 100% man while being 100% God? What a mystery! All of this caused the visitors to watch in a quiet hush.

Once "Mary" had discreetly covered little "Jesus" with a privacy blan-ket and he . . . or she had had her fill . . . there would be no other noises except for the occasional cow's moo or sheep blat. Those coming through the scene were overcome with the reality of all of this. One elderly woman stood transfixed looking at the child, tears streaming down her face. It was, after all, quite a fact to wrap your mind around . . . that the very God of the universe had willingly chosen to leave the splendor of heaven to come down to earth to sleep in a smelly barn and take on human form . . . just so you and I could receive grace. There it was again . . . grace . . . it seemed to be at the center of everything saturating the theme of the carols. Brad who was playing the part of Joseph began to quietly sing a verse of an old carol: *"Down in a lowly manger, The humble Christ was born, And God sent us salvation, that blessed Christmas morn."* Looking at the baby Hannah . . . grace . . . wrapped up in her mother's arms, Brad was overcome. "Yes indeed," he mused, "Christmas was really all about grace . . . about receiving gifts you don't deserve." He wiped his eyes, pretending it was the lights bothering him.

At the end of the three nights, over two thousand visitors had come and experienced this wonderful event. According to the local papers, never had Knox Country seen anything quite like this. Once again, the light of the glorious gospel had shed its light on the people of mid-coast Maine. Harold could only wonder how this would affect those who came, saw, and contemplated the unspeakable gift sent from heaven to earth.

Chapter 35

Oops, Somebody Forgot to . . .

Glancing at his buzzing cell phone, Hal recognized the number. It was Brad, a young man who was growing dearer and closer to him every day. This was Hal's first year as a full-time pastor, and it hadn't turned out as he had anticipated. He thought it would be all about preaching and teaching but to his amazement he could now describe the vast majority of his time and energy with one word: People.

Although public speaking was one of his passions . . . Hal was coming to terms with something he had read by the late Joe Aldrich: "People won't care how much you know . . . until they know how much you care." Wow . . . was that right on! He thought it would be his sermons that would help mold and encourage his flock . . . but it was the relational part of ministry that seemed to be a priority. Pushing the "talk" button Hal exuberantly answered: "Hey friend, what's up?" If he could meet him at the coffee nook in the Owl and Turtle Bookshop, he would find out. It seemed pretty urgent . . . almost with a tone of panic. Hal had just finished a visit at the hospital and could be there in fifteen minutes.

He found Brad sitting at a corner table sporting a somber look. "Want a cup of Joe?" inquired Hal. "Hmmm . . . " pondered Brad, "sounds great. I need something to pick me up. Thanks . . . black with two sugars please." Coming back to the booth Hal sat across from Brad and began stirring his hot coffee. Looking at his young friend Hal mustered a fatherly tone: "You like you've lost your best friend. What's up?"

Looking out of the front window, Brad began: "Best friend . . . well maybe. I feel like Sam's my best friend . . . as well as my future wife. I am not quite sure. I was in town yesterday and I saw her sitting in the diner . . . with a guy . . . a very young, handsome, guy. I called her later on her cell and it rang and rang . . . like she didn't want to talk to me. I am not sure what to do . . . I don't know if a May wedding is still in the works . . . or what in the heck is happening?" Brad's voice trailed off, his face dropping into his hands as he sat, despondent.

Hal sat back with his hands folded behind his head . . . thinking. He took a couple of sips of his coffee and then spoke. "I am certainly no expert on women. There are lots of things I don't understand like quantum physics, cricket, the stock market . . . but above all . . . women! I can tell you this. I am a pretty good judge of character, and I don't think Samantha is duplicitous . . . by that, I don't think she would ever intentionally live a double life . . . or try to hide stuff from you.

She may be afraid of hurting you or even losing you . . . and is just taking some time to tell you about something. Why don't you go with your heart? You love her . . . she loves you . . . and you both love little Hannah . . . so act normal and give her lots of opportunities to talk. Take her out." "Yeah," replied Brad . . . " I guess we haven't done a lot together lately what with me working at church and running to classes . . . and late assignments and papers to write." Hal winked . . . "Hey . . . I just remembered something. Remember that old guitar you sold Billy Simms? Well, I ran into him in the Pen Bay cafeteria this morning and he handed me an envelope for you." Brad's eyes lit up. Raising both hands, he gave Hal two thumbs up and proclaimed "Dude!" that's a hundred bucks! Score! Olive Garden here we come!" Harold stood and dug down in his back pocket for the folded envelope, which he passed to a now cheerful Brad. "Let me know how things work out with Sam. I am sure there is a perfectly good explanation."

Over supper, Hal explained it all to Liz who narrowed her eyebrows in a scowl. "I can't imagine her two-timing, Brad. There's way too much on the line here . . . especially for little Hannah. Do you think we should have a "cup of tea" and a heart-to-heart?" "Hmm?" pondered Harold. "What do you say we give this some time and see how this shakes down? Let's let things run their course.

January in Maine was "snappin cold" with morning temperatures running in the teens. At 8 a.m. Hal kissed Liz on the cheek and announced in his best Maine accent: *Big day Mothah . . . Got a wicked good sehmon up my sleeve and don't forget . . . we got us a baptism this monin!"* And just like that the reverend Harold B. Tuttle was out the door and off to prepare in his office. Liz watched through the back window and had a good chuckle when Hal almost went airborne when he stepped on an icy spot wearing only dress shoes.

Giggling, Liz was startled by a loud "Woof" behind her. "Oh, Walter . . . sorry I forgot to put you out. Better get your tinkles done before the parking lot fills up!" Walter waited patiently by the kitchen door. As she swung the door open to let the big dog out, it knocked a startled Samantha on the knee. "Sorry honey! You OK?" Samantha laughed and declared: "These boots are like armor!" Puzzled, Liz inquired as to why she was there so early and where was her precious bundle? "Hannah's with mom over at the church. She is as nervous as a cat at a dog show! You know she's getting baptized today? Can you believe it . . . my mom . . . getting baptized?" Liz laughed as she ushered her into the warm kitchen. "Sit down dear. How can I help you?" "Well . . . I know you've got to get going but I needed to tell you about something."

Strumming his guitar, Brad seemed to be in excellent form. The church was full and as Harold sat on what he jokingly referred to as the "the archbishop's throne," he surveyed the crowd. In the back row, he noticed Brenda, and her former husband John who had driven up from Boston, Samantha, holding little Hannah and sitting next to her was a tall, good-looking young man. A chill went up his spine. How could she dare do this? And right here in church? How in the world?

Hal kept an eye on Brad, wondering when he would take notice. There had never been a fistfight here in church . . . but maybe this was the day? Brad seemed undeterred and maintained a calm, even joyful composure. After the third worship song, Brad invited the church family to take a moment and greet one another. Placing his guitar in its stand, Brad headed toward the back of the church. Hal almost jumped off the stage with enthusiasm. Brad headed to the back left corner of the sanctuary and without any hesitation gave Samantha, Hannah, and Brenda a peck on the cheek and squeezed John's hand. Brad turned to the young man and Hal held his breath. He extended his hand, clasped him on the shoulder, and said: "Dave, I'm so glad you came today."

The young man smiled and turned to Harold who had come back out of curiosity. "Hello Pastor, I'm Dave Phillips . . . I am," he blushed, "Samantha's former boyfriend." Hal extended his hand. "Dave, welcome . . . do you live here?" The young man explained: "Well sir, I attend Boston College. I used to work up here and that's when I met Samantha. She can fill you in

. . . suffice it to say I have not always been very kind or considerate to her . . . and I am here because of grace! And I am so happy for her and Brad, it's the best thing for little Hannah too . . . " Now Samantha was crying and blowing her nose. She leaned over to her pastor and said: "I'll explain later . . . if that's OK?" Hal smiled and gave her a reassuring squeeze. "Well, Dave we all have something in common. If it were not for grace . . . none of us would be here . . . so you're in good company . . . and I'm glad you are here."

As he walked back toward his seat, a light came on in Hal's brain. Dave must be the young man Samantha had told them about . . . the student who was the father of her child. He must have had second thoughts about Samantha . . . and on his school break from Boston decided to talk with her. The meeting Brad had witnessed at the diner must have been about his change of heart. Now Hal realized why Brad was so upbeat . . . even congenial toward the child's father. They had worked it all out. With Brad's proposal young Dave was "off the hook." Even though it was noble of him to try to set things right, it certainly made more sense for Sam and Hannah to be with Brad. He loved them both without reservation. A great sense of relief washed over Harold. Now he finally "got it!"

The service got back under way and soon Harold had launched out into his sermon on the story of Philip and the Ethiopian official from the book of Acts. At the end of his sermon, Hal paused. "It was pretty simple. The Ethiopian believed in Jesus and asked the question: "Look there is water, what is there to prevent me from being baptized? The answer was simple: Nothing! Let's do it.

Today Brenda Gifford has come to us. Like the man in our text, she also has come to faith . . . and as our church has a baptistery full of water . . . some believers sprinkle, some pour but here in our church we dunk . . . just like Jesus did in the Jordan . . . so let's do it!" A thunderous applause came up from the congregation. While Brad led the congregation with a couple of worship songs Hal slipped into his office. Opening the closet door, he unhooked a green pair of L.L.Bean hip waders. Leon Bean would have never guessed that his rubber waders would become a favorite of clergy from coast to coast.

The deacons had folded back the doors on the stage floor that gave access to the steps that led down into an eight-by-five-foot fiberglass baptismal tank. A microphone had been set in front of the tank so the congregation could hear all. Everything had been arranged . . . except for one very important detail. A baptistery should be filled with heated water in the winter. Overnight the outside temperatures had dipped to below zero and the unheated tank's bottom was exposed to the freezing cold in the ancient unheated basement. To say the water in the tank was "arctic" would have been an understatement. Pastor Tuttle, stepping down into the water, sensed it was chilly . . . but protected by the thick hip waders, had no idea just how cold the water was. Now standing waist high in the tank, Harold looked to the back of the church and beaconed a white-robed Brenda to come forward.

As she made her way forward, the pianist played softly, and Betsy Dinsmore readied herself with a pile of towels in which she would help a freshly baptized Brenda both dry off and maintain modesty. When wet, the white baptismal robes tended to reveal more than necessary, creating a spectacle especially appreciated and anticipated by the gawking teenage boys perched on the balcony.

Harold began: "Today brothers and sisters we are blessed to have our new sister Brenda Gifford make a public declaration about her newfound faith . . . by joining me here in the waters of baptism."

Samantha and John had now moved to the front pew. John proudly held his pink-dressed granddaughter while Samantha fiddled with a camera and blew her nose.

Harold moved to the stairs and extended his hand. Brenda took it and tentatively took her first step into the water. She gasped. Not understanding what the problem was, Hal simply tried to reassure her by saying "It's OK dear . . . I've got you." Brenda hesitated. Hal waited. She felt her toes go numb in the frigid water. She took a second step . . . and gasped loudly. Harold reassured her again. Brenda clenched her teeth and took a third step. Her breathing grew louder and she began to shake. Hal, not in touch with the situation simply continued coaxing. When she took the fourth step, the icy water rushed up to what one refers to as "The water line." She could bear it no more. Poor dear Brenda opened her mouth and screeched! Harold held her right hand tightly as she bounced back and forth on her tippy toes. A murmur rose from the startled congregation.

Dick Maurice ran across the stage and bending over, dipped his hands in the water exclaiming: *"We forgot to heat the watah last night! It's as cold as Damariscotta Pond!"* "Coldah!" bellowed Brenda. Harold shouted over the din: "Let's get this poor girl baptized before she gets hypothermia!" As Brenda took her last step the cold water unmercifully hit her kidneys. She screeched again. Grabbing her by the shoulders, Harold spoke loudly above the roar of the crowd: "Brenda, based upon your profession of faith in Christ, I baptize you in the name of the Father, the Son, and the Holy Spirit." With that, he plunged the Brenda into the icy water. Now, with his arms fully immersed, Hal understood . . . and wasted no time pulling her up to the surface. Brenda gasped loudly and leaped out of the water into the arms of Betsy Dinsmore, nearly knocking her over. Betsy, regaining her balance began wrapping towels around the shaking Brenda. Hal whispered to Betsy and Liz: "Hurry! Get her dry . . . and get some hot coffee or tea into her before she catches pneumonia!"

Brad led the nearly hysterical congregation into one last chorus. Pastor Harold, now standing, dripped onto the carpet. Raising his hand, he gave a short pastoral benediction and headed off to change in his office. This was Harold B. Tuttle's first baptism as the new pastor of Appleton Community Church . . . and it would not soon be forgotten. In the years to follow, Brenda would speak in excited tones describing her "Arctic plunge of faith!"

Chapter 36

A Lesson From a Needlepoint

Hal sat pondering the events of the past couple of months. He struggled to articulate his thoughts, so instead of babbling, he simply sipped his coffee, letting his mind drift. This morning was quiet and peaceful. Liz sat on the sofa with her feet curled under her. Walter, his four black paws sticking straight up had claimed the remainder of the sofa.

Softly humming, she worked quietly on her cross-stitch project taking an occasional sip from her hot cocoa. Harold, across the room in his leather armchair, worked to identify the shapes and colors of her canvas and tilted his head to the right . . . and then to the left trying to make out what Liz was making. Finally, he spoke: "Liz . . . have you any idea what kind of a mess I see from here? What in the world are you making?" Liz smiled and turned the wooden hoop around. "It's a gift for baby Hannah's room." It's called a "Noah's Ark Sampler."

Now that Harold could see it clearly, he was impressed. Thousands of tiny needlepoint stitches had been used to create Noah's ark and its many animals delicately stitched in full color and all exiting the ark. Behind the ark was the banner of a rainbow. In the center were the words: "Hannah, God's Gift of Grace." "Wow hon . . . that's awesome. That must have taken you forever?" "Well, not forever but at least three months." Then she turned it around, offering Hal the rearview again. Thousands of colored strings went in all directions. Compared to the beauty of the front, it was not attractive.

Hal, suddenly overcome with emotion jumped up, stepped across the room, and gave a surprised Liz an enthusiastic smack on the cheek. "Wow

. . . I didn't know you were into needlepoint?" Hal dropped back into the armchair as if hit by a sack of bricks. "That's it!" he proclaimed. It's all in your point of view. Liz put her feet down, sat up straight, and said "Huh?"

"Now I understand! I have been totally confused about what God has been up to. Samantha . . . Brad . . . the letter . . . John and Brenda . . . it all seemed like such a mess. Because I could not see what God was up to. Just like your needlepoint, I have only been seeing the back . . . the mess . . . the horrible, twisted mess of strings . . . going in a thousand directions . . . was just plain ugly . . . and I couldn't figure it out. I've been confused by the strings! You knew all along what you were doing! And while I didn't "get it," God has been creating something of infinite beauty! I just needed a change of perspective.

"Hmm" mused Liz. "Didn't Paul remind the Christians in Rome that all of these things work together for our good. "Right, you are Mrs. Tuttle. You preach . . . I'll turn the pages!

Chapter 37

The Big Reveal

The long winter behind them, tulips blossomed, and the lawns, pasture-land, and forests turned varying shades of green. Along the coastline, wildflowers sprung up from among the rocks. Now into the first week of May, locals had shed their flannel shirts and "bean" boots donning t-shirts, shorts, and sandals. Window frames, fences, and houses received a fresh coat of paint, giving them renewed color and vibrancy.

Along the coastal villages, previously vacant boat slips now housed all manner of marine craft. Summer was in view and the regulars from "away" were up preparing their boats and cabins for another glorious summer on the coast of Maine. Restaurants and shops came out of hibernation and were once again open for business. Camden Harbor was abuzz with the tinkling of dishes and silverware as busy servers delivered meals at an astounding rate of speed. Students hustled and broke a sweat knowing their income was seasonal. "Making hay while the sun shines" is a way of life for those in Maine's tourist industry.

With spring comes a fresh attitude about life in general. Flowers get planted, plants potted, lawns manicured, and hedges trimmed as sunshine and warmth become the norm. Arriving on the swelling tide of activity is a flurry of weddings, reunions, and lawn parties . . . all requiring copious floral deliveries.

This Saturday, large red and white bouquets were being carried into the Appleton Community Church from the back of a long silver van proclaiming "Spauldings Floral Shop" on its sides. With a two o'clock wedding on the schedule, there would be no room for error. The floral delivery team set the massive arrangements in their appointed places while both in the sanctuary and fellowship hall a group of boisterous ladies were aflutter hanging ribbons, positioning candles, silver place settings, and covering tables.

Today represented the culmination of one of the greatest stories of love and grace this congregation . . . and this community had ever witnessed. There would be no empty seats. The entire church was invited along with family and friends from four other states. Two men were busy positioning video cameras and monitors to provide the overflow crowd with an audio and video feed to the educational building. In his office the Reverend Harold B. Tuttle went over and over his notes while, Walter, his faithful Poodle sidekick seemed undisturbed by the stress of the day and lay on his back, feet sticking straight up, snoring.

At one-thirty, Liz showed up at Hal's office in a stunning, peach-colored dress. Hal took her in . . . sitting in silence. "If I weren't the pastor of this church . . . and you didn't mind getting your makeup messed up . . . well, my dear, I would smooch you right here and now!" Liz giggled like a schoolgirl. Leaning over him she whispered: "Focus dear . . . focus. You have a wedding in thirty minutes!" As she exited the room she looked back, grinned, and said "Hmm . . . maybe a smooch later?" Hal threw a crumpled sticky note at her as he hissed: "Temptress!"

By two o'clock the church was packed. The wedding party in place, Hal nodded at Marion Potter to begin the organ prelude. A few latecomers were quickly escorted to their seats. Together, the organ and the piano began to play a piece by Pachelbel's Canon in D. Hal thought to himself: "Oh dear, Samantha's going to be crying." He checked under the pulpit. As requested, Ruth had placed a fresh box of Kleenex tissues there. There were two hundred and fifty in this box. Hal hoped it would be enough.

The bridesmaids, best man, and wedding party slowly and solemnly entered. Liz followed carrying baby Hannah dressed in a matching little peach dress. The crowd "oohed and awed" enthusiastically. When they were in place Hal nodded again at the musicians as he gave the signal for all to stand. Down the aisle came a sight that had never been seen before in Appleton Community Church. Two couples came arm in arm . . . John and Brenda . . . followed by Brad and Samantha.

Standing, the congregation was speechless. Hal asked the crowd to sit and stepped up to the microphone. "Today, dear friends we have the opportunity to witness an unparalleled event. I checked our church records and we have never had a double wedding before. This is a first. I don't usually give a lot of details about the circumstances surrounding a wedding . . . but I have been requested to do so by the family . . . because it will give glory to God. I also commend the wedding party for their transparency. I will be sharing some very personal details . . . but you will soon understand why.

When I first met Samantha, we had no idea what she was going through. God happened to have our paths cross on a bitterly cold night on the Rockland breakwater. She had made a grave error in judgment and found herself with child and was contemplating ending her life, as well as her babies. Her mother, having just gone through a messy divorce had asked her to leave her home. She was ready to end her life by drowning. Samantha pondered her future, as to whether God could forgive her or any man could ever love her. On that long breakwater, we had a divine appointment. We simply embraced her and tried to help her find warmth and shelter . . . literally. Well, God wonderfully provided a good solution, and she moved in with Gladys Berry." By now Samantha's mascara was beginning to run and was, along with her mother and father unable to stem the flow of tears. All over the church, there was nose-blowing and eye-wiping.

"I know it all sounds a bit like a fairytale, but God made Himself very real to Samantha . . . and worked in the heart of our own Brad Everett." Hal looked at Brad who was working on a very crooked "Charlie Brown" smile. Hal smiled at Brad, knowing just what that smile felt like. "Anyhow, Samantha fell in love with a God of grace and forgiveness . . . and not long after, Brad and Samantha fell in love with each other." In the third row, the elderly Gladys Berry raised her hands and shouted, "Thank you Jesus!" which brought a chorus of "amens" and laughter from the congregation.

Now, wiping his eyes, Pastor Harold continued: "Samantha could never have imagined that all the while she was discovering faith and forgiveness, her father, John Gifford was being drawn to Jesus through a church outside Boston. As he grew in his faith, he became aware of two things: he needed to reestablish his broken relationship with Samantha and share his newfound grace with his ex-wife Brenda. Well . . . you might remember the day that Brenda took her icy plunge here at church in January." With that, the crowd laughed loudly. Many wiped tears from their eyes and blew their nose. With the break in the silence, Samantha also took the opportunity to blow her nose loudly. Smiling, Brad leaned over and gave her a gentle kiss on the cheek.

"Today," Hal continued, "is a day of redemption. It is a day of grace, of unmerited favor. It is all about reconciliation. God loves to redeem lost people. He loves to repair broken relationships . . . especially broken marriages." Walking over to Liz he held his hands out and took little Hannah to his chest. "Today friends, is a day of hope . . . of a future . . . of a new life as this family now walks hand in hand with Jesus."

Newlyweds . . . or re-newlyweds John and Brenda Gifford held their precious little Hannah and waved goodbye to Brad and Samantha who were now headed down Appleton Road, tin cans clanging in the distance.

In the late afternoon shadows, Hal and Liz walked hand in hand without speaking. A little over a year ago they had wondered why God had led them here. Today the Master had turned his "divine needlepoint" around, revealing a surprising work of grace . . . a masterpiece of breath-taking beauty in a place called Appleton, Maine.

The End

www.ingramcontent.com/pod-product-compliance
Lightning Source LLC
Chambersburg PA
CBHW071226260626
47162CB00004B/1442